A BOTTLE IN THE GAZA SEA

By Valérie Zenatti

When I Was a Soldier

A Bottle in the Gaza Sea

A BOTTLE IN THE GAZA SEA

VALÉRIE ZENATTI

TRANSLATED BY ADRIANA HUNTER

BLOOMSBURY

NEW YORK BERLIN LONDON

Published by Bloomsbury Books for Young Readers
175 Fifth Avenue, New York, New York 10010

This book is supported by the French Ministry of Foreign Affairs as part of the
Burgess program run by the Cultural Department of the French Embassy in
London (www.frenchbooknews.com)

Liberté · Égalité · Fraternité
RÉPUBLIQUE FRANÇAISE

Library of Congress Cataloging-in-Publication Data
Zenatti, Valérie.
[Bouteille dans la Mer de Gaza. English]
A bottle in the Gaza Sea / by Valerie Zenatti ; translated by Adriana Hunter.—
1st U.S. ed.
p.   cm.
Summary: Seventeen-year-old Tal Levine of Jerusalem, despondent over the
ongoing Arab-Israeli conflict, puts her hopes for peace in a bottle and asks
her brother, a military nurse in the Gaza Strip, to toss it into the sea, leading
ultimately to friendship and understanding between her and an "enemy."
ISBN-13: 978-1-59990-200-5 • ISBN-10: 1-59990-200-1
1. Arab-Israeli conflict—Juvenile fiction
[1. Arab-Israeli conflict—Fiction. 2. Toleration—Fiction. 3. Letters—Fiction.
4. Israel—Fiction. 5. Gaza Strip—Fiction.]
I. Hunter, Adriana. II. Title.
PZ7.Z425Bot 2008   [Fic]—dc22   2007042361

First U.S. Edition April 2008
Typeset by Dorchester Typesetting Group Ltd.
Printed in the United States by Thomson-Shore, Inc. Dexter, Michigan
4 6 8 10 9 7 5

For the luminous Sophie and Jérôme

*Ce n'est pas parce que les uns ont raison que
les autres ont tort. Il faut garder les rêves intacts.
Les rêves, c'est ce qui nous fait avancer.*

It is not because some people are right that others
are wrong. All of our dreams must remain intact. Our
dreams keep us moving forward.

Jerusalem, September 9, 2003

It's a time of darkness, sadness, and horror. The fear's back again.

Mom had just told me to go to bed for the third time (because I have to get up early in the mornings) when the windows started rattling. My heart gave a great thump inside my chest; I thought it had come halfway up my throat. A second later I realized there had been an explosion really close to our house.

An explosion must mean a bomb.

My older brother, Eytan, who's a military nurse, ran straight out with his first aid kit. Dad hesitated for a moment, then followed him. Mom held me in her arms and cried; then, as usual, she did four things at once: she turned on the TV and the radio, connected to the Internet, and grabbed her cell phone. That's what I call a highly technological response.

I ran to my bedroom, confident that no one would nag me to switch off my light and that the next day I could even get to school late, or not go at all. Nobody would ask for an explanation. I would just have to say the bomb was in my neighborhood, in my street, I had nightmares all night, my blood pressure soared, I couldn't walk, I was too frightened to leave the house. And Mrs. Barzilaï would believe me, even if we had a math test.

A few minutes after the explosion we heard the ambulance sirens—such a horrible noise, ripping through the air and our eardrums. A terrible yowling like a cat with its tail caught in a door, amplified by a sound system worthy of a hard rock concert. Five, six, seven ambulances, but I didn't count them all.

I can hear Mom still on the phone, and the clear staccato voice of some woman correspondent on the radio or the TV. There will have been some deaths. There are almost always deaths. But I don't want to know how many, or who. Not today. Precisely because it happened so close to home.

I'd like to turn the silence right up, but how do you do that?

I went into the kitchen to drink a bit of vodka and lemon. Mom didn't see me. On my way I picked up the earplugs Dad uses when he goes swimming. With those plus my big pillow over my head I might have some hope of sleeping, even if I know that when I wake up tomorrow no one will tell me that everything's fine and it's all been a bad dream.

The vodka didn't go down very well. Half a glass is obviously too much for me. This morning I had a headache and my face was all swollen. "You look like Bugs Bunny," Eytan told me, ruffling my hair. My brother's the only person in the world who can mess up my hair without being walloped within a second. He knows that and makes the most of it.

He smiled at me. He didn't look like someone who'd spent the night witnessing horror, but then what do you look like when you've witnessed horror? He's twenty years old and doing military service in Gaza; I'm sure he sees terrible things there every day . . . or every other day, when it's quiet. I expect he'd have to learn to not see, or at least to forget, if he wants to avoid looking old before he's twenty-five.

It's strange, I don't think I've ever written as much as I have between yesterday and today. There are some girls in my class who keep diaries and write down what happens to them every day. I've never done that—dissected my love life, or said how old and useless my parents are, or divulged my dreams. Well, I imagine that's what you put in a diary.

On my thirteenth birthday my grandmother gave me *The Diary of Anne Frank*, the story of the young Jewish girl in the Netherlands who spent two years of her life hiding with her family during the Second World War before being deported. She dreamed of being a writer, but more important, of freedom: to go to the cinema, to walk in a garden, to look at the trees and listen to the birds without fear of

3

being caught and killed by the Nazis. There was another family in the hiding place with a son named Peter, and Anne fell in love with him. I've often wondered whether she really loved him or whether she didn't have any choice because he was the only boy there.

What upset me most was the end of the book where it said: Anne Frank died two months before the camp at Bergen-Belsen was liberated.

Just two months . . . I read that sentence again and again, and for a long time I wished I could reach out, take Anne Frank's hand, and say, "Hang on, this hell is nearly over, it won't go on forever, just eight little weeks. Hang on and you'll be free, you'll be able to go to the cinema, to look at the trees and listen to the birds; you could even be a writer. Please, live!"

But I don't have superpowers or a time machine, and that's what's so heartbreaking when you think about it.

I still don't know why I'm writing all this. I get average grades for literature, nothing more, and I have no dreams of being a writer. What I really want is to make films, to be a director. Or perhaps a pediatrician, I haven't really chosen yet. But, since yesterday evening, I've got this incredible urge to write; it's all I can think about. As if there's a river of words bursting to come out of me to keep me alive. I feel as if I'll never be able to stop.

I haven't managed to avoid the news. My eyes see, my ears hear, there are newspapers and radios everywhere, and they keep talking about the bomb attack.

The terrorist blew himself up inside the Hillel café. They found six bodies. It's what they call an average attack, which means it will be talked about for a couple of days and then there will be a bit more in the Sunday supplements. There was a tragedy, a tragedy within the tragedy: a young woman was killed with her father. She was due to be married today. She was killed a few hours before putting on her beautiful white dress, a few hours before the photographer took the young couple to the loveliest places in Jerusalem to take pictures of the prince and princess who would have lots of children. The groom-who-never-got-married was devastated by the sight of her coffin. He wanted to put the wedding ring on his fiancée's finger but the rabbi refused, saying religious law forbade celebrating a union with a dead person.

I wonder whether religious law devotes a chapter to how to behave when you're in the depths of despair.

I close my eyes to forget the face of that girl who'll never be married. She was just twenty, barely three years older than me. What would my life be like if I knew I only had three years left? I have no idea—it's a stupid, pointless question but I still can't stop thinking about it.

When the fear comes back, like now, we all seem to forget who we are. We all become potential victims, bodies that could end up lifeless and covered in blood just because someone chose to blow themselves up right next to us. I want to know who I am, what I'm made of. What would make my death any different from any other? If I said that to my parents or friends, they'd be really shocked and would tell me gently that I needed to rest. That must be why I've decided to write: so I don't frighten the others with what's going on inside my head . . . and don't let them declare me a raving lunatic.

Seeing Doves Fly

My name is Tal Levine. I was born in Tel Aviv on the first of July 1986, but I live here in Jerusalem. I know that everyone on the planet knows the name Jerusalem, and if there are extraterrestrials they've probably heard about it too; it's a city that creates quite a stir. But no one knows it like my father and me. My father is passionate about history and archaeology, and he's one of Israel's greatest tour guides. When a head of state visits, he's the one they call on because he brings the stones to life with his stories. He's a magician. He has limpid green eyes, and this strange gleam appears in them when he starts talking about how King David chose to put the capital of his kingdom on this rocky mountain such a long way from the sea or a river, how his son Solomon built a temple and palaces, how Nebuchadnezzar, then the Romans, destroyed the temple. He can talk for hours about Jesus, who looked over Jerusalem from the cross.

"Do you realize, Tal," he often says, "this is where all that happened and this is where everything still will happen." He explains how, much later, European crusaders fought the Muslims to reclaim Jesus' tomb. And then there were the long centuries when this Holy City fell from splendor. The Old Town, a tiny place stifled by its city walls, was all there was until a hundred years ago. "Dark little streets," my father says, "streets where a donkey could bump into a man without wondering whether he was a Jew, a Christian, or a Muslim. Several thousand good, pious people watched over the sacred sites of the three religions, thinking they were the last to remember them, and that as the world moved into a modern era, people would forget that Jerusalem is the center of the universe. They were wrong. When the Jews chose to come back to the land of their ancestors to be a free people, rivalries over the city began to simmer. The Jews said they'd been here first, three thousand years earlier, that it was written in the Bible, and that, in the two thousand years when they had had no country, all their prayers had been turned toward Jerusalem. The Muslims replied that they had been there for thirteen centuries, which is not really to be sneezed at, and that their prophet Muhammad had flown to the skies from here. The Christians tried to get their word in, reminding the others that Jesus died here, and should he ever come back to life, there was a strong chance it would be in the same place so it would be a good idea to have a few of them on the spot to welcome him. But you see, Tal, instead of loving this city in the way it deserves,

8

instead of getting along, they've fought over her for more than fifty years, the way men might once have fought for a woman, with passion, with a little more hate for their rivals every day. They don't even realize their wars are now damaging the thing they claim to love, damaging it more and more violently in one way or another."

That's how my father talks. That's what makes him a wonderful poet, a storyteller. I could walk with him for hours, traveling through time, looking at my city through eyes different from most people's. I know there are amazing cities in the world. I would love to see Paris, Venice, Beijing, and New York, but I already know that this is where I want to live.

To live, and not to die.

I'm back on the subject now. I can't think about anything else at the moment, I can't forget the fact that the bomb was so close to home.

A few years ago I went walking by the Dead Sea with my father and Eytan. I fell and cut myself very badly. It was a really frightening, ugly wound, but I couldn't take my eyes off the blood, off that long opening from my knee to my ankle that made me feel as if my leg were no longer my leg.

I've got exactly the same feeling now, except that I'm all in one piece. But inside my head, I'm in pieces. I keep thinking how often I go to the Hillel café, with Eytan when he's on leave, or with my friends. I keep thinking we could have been there. I don't understand how life can hinge on so little: whether or not you feel like going to the café along a certain street.

9

There has been an incalculable number of bomb attacks in Jerusalem in the last three years. Sometimes it's every day, or even twice a day. You can't keep up with the funerals on TV or crying for the families, there are too many of them.

People say they get used to it. Not me.

I grew up with the idea that there could be something other than blood, hate, and mutilated bodies between us and the Palestinians.

I was seven years old in 1993, but I remember the thirteenth of September really clearly. Mom and Dad didn't go to work, they bought tons of chips, little sausages, pistachio nuts, and champagne too. Their eyes sparkled and they kept the TV on the whole time but couldn't sit still in front of it.

It's very rare for the TV to be on in the daytime.

It's even rarer for my parents to buy junk food.

It's incredibly rare for them to let us, Eytan and me, stuff our faces with crap and not say anything.

And it's seriously unbelievable that they gave me, aged seven, champagne to drink.

It's probably because of all that that I remember the thirteenth of September 1993 so well. On the screen, standing in front of a palace made of icing sugar, was our prime minister, Yitzhak Rabin. Next to him was some guy who looked like an actor from an American soap opera. In fact it was the president of the United States, Bill Clinton. He took Yitzhak Rabin by the shoulder and led him to a weird man with a black and white checkered scarf over his head. I gathered from what the commentator was saying that this was Yasser Arafat, representing the Palestinians. The two men shook hands, and all those thousands of people in their best clothes standing on the White House lawn (it said on the screen: Live from the White House) clapped as if this were some fantastic achievement.

That was when I saw my parents cry for the first time. I was very embarrassed, and I think I was annoyed with them. There they were with these inexplicable tears in their eyes, looking like little children, and I felt like saying, "You'd better get back to being you quickly—I don't mind if you're serious, strict, or gentle, but just get back to being my parents. Parents don't cry, as far as I know. They know everything, they're very dependable and very strong, they don't just start crying ridiculously because they see two men shaking hands."

I also remember being very frightened because, if my parents were crying, that meant something awful had happened and our life was going to change. The champagne, the chips, the little sausages, and the pistachio nuts must have been brought in to celebrate our last moments together, or some other dramatic, irreversible event.

Dad looked at me.

"Come over here, Tal."

He sat me on his knee, stroked my face, and said, "People sometimes cry with happiness, sweetheart. And we're very, very happy today. What you've just seen is very important: the Palestinians and us, the Israelis, are finally going to agree about how to live in peace. There won't be any more war, ever. Maybe you and Eytan won't even have to do national

11

service. This is the most overwhelming piece of news because we've dreamed of it for so long."

He believed in it, my father. And, as I believe everything he tells me, that at least made two of us who saw white doves flying through the skies above Jerusalem that day.

A Letter, a Bottle, Some Hope

It happened this morning, during Mrs. Feldman's biology lesson. How do ideas happen? In cartoons a bulb lights up. *Bling!* The hero smiles, he's pleased, like God in the Bible on the first day of the Creation, he wanted there to be light and there was light. But I wasn't hoping for anything; I didn't feel particularly in the dark. I was listening attentively to Mrs. Feldman explaining genetics, taking peas as her example. I thought it was funny, picturing a Mr. Pea and a Mrs. Pea who decide to have children and worry whether they'll be small and smooth or fat and wrinkled, and most important whether they will taste good. Then all of a sudden I heard inside my head: "I've got to send what I've written to someone." It was my silent voice, the one we all have, the voice inside our heads when we're thinking. Maybe what Mrs. Feldman was saying woke it up—something like "genetics allows for detailed studies of similarities and differences in individuals of the same species, and for comparisons of different species."

Then there was quite a hubbub because Dov, the class joker, put up his hand to ask a question. Mrs. Feldman was delighted to see him joining in the lesson for once and she turned toward him, tilting her chin and smiling encouragingly.

"Yes, Dov?"

"While we're on the subject, Mrs. Feldman, do you know what's small, round, and goes up and down in an elevator?"

The whole class burst out laughing, and Mrs. Feldman, who didn't seem to know the joke or had forgotten it thirty years ago, got angry.

I heard the voice again: "Yes, that's it, someone's got to read it, on the other side."

In the next lesson, which was history, I didn't listen to anything because I was so excited. I was writing but not taking notes. Efrat, my best-friend-who-always-sits-next-to-me, whispered, "What are you doing?"

"I'm writing a letter," I replied, putting one hand over the piece of paper.

"Who to?"

"To . . . to Ori," I stammered.

"Ori?" she said, raising one incredulous eyebrow. "But you saw him yesterday and you'll see him later at lunch! Anyway, you never write to each other."

That's the problem with best friends: you tell them everything and share everything with them, and in the end you can't have a square inch of secret garden without them turning into superspies from the FBI, digging up the soil until they find a bone.

"Well, you see, I realized there was stuff we couldn't say to each other and it would be easier to write," I replied, more confidently this time.

Her face lit up.

"Is it a breakup letter?"

I shot her a nasty look and told her that if I were writing a breakup letter to Ori I would be sobbing, and that I couldn't understand why the idea of it made her so happy. She shrugged her shoulders, slightly annoyed, just as the history teacher (who always thinks he's so spiritual) snapped at us, "Hey, you two gossips, this isn't the market, is it? You can sharpen your forked tongues after my lesson, please."

I hate teachers who think that chatty girls are gossips and chatty boys just need to let off a bit of steam. Rosebush is one of them. (Obviously, our history teacher isn't called Rosebush, but Rosenbaum. Mom told me it meant Rosebush in German. Efrat and I laughed about it for two whole days, and it's been his official nickname at school ever since.)

The whole class cracked up. I hated them for it. Especially the girls. But it just shows that female solidarity doesn't stand up to a misogynist teacher's bad jokes.

Efrat turned toward the blackboard, looking as if she were concentrating, and I was finally free to start my letter, which I've pasted in here.

Dear you,

If you ever read this letter you'll already know a few

things about me: my name, how old I am, my father's job, my best friend's name, and even my history teacher's nickname.

But I don't know anything about you.

I imagine you with long dark hair, hazel eyes, and—I'm not sure why—a dreamy expression.

I imagine you're often sad.

I imagine you're the same age as me, but I don't know whether, at seventeen, you feel very old or very young.

I imagine your heart beating faster sometimes, but when and for whom?

I imagine that, like me, you wonder who you will be in ten years and that you can't see anything specific.

I imagine you have younger brothers who annoy you, but that you love them all the same.

And maybe you have an older brother you adore, like me.

You see, I started writing these pages just after the bomb went off near my house. I can still hear that terrible boom, and not an hour goes by when I don't see the smiling face and smooth hair of the girl who was supposed to get married.

You must know that every time there's a bomb everyone wonders how the Palestinians can do it, killing innocent people. I've often wondered myself.

And then I thought that it was meaningless saying "the Palestinians." That it must be the same with you as it is with us, there must be fat people and thin people, rich and poor, good people and bastards.

I'm full of fear and full of hope writing to you like this. I've never written to someone I didn't know. It feels strange. I'm not sure I'll manage to say what I want to say.

Maybe you'll tear up this letter and the pages with it. Maybe you feel nothing but hate when you hear the word Israel. Maybe you'll laugh at me. Or maybe you just don't exist.

But if this letter is lucky enough to reach you, if you're patient enough to read it to the end, if—like me—you think we should learn to know each other, for all sorts of reasons but mainly because we want to get on with living our lives in peace because we're young . . . then send me a reply.

I can't seem to say any more. I don't know if what I'm doing is good or bad, crazy or just eccentric, useful or pointless.

I'm going to put all this in a bottle, the one we drank on the thirteenth of September 1993. Mom and Dad were keeping it as a souvenir of that great event, but never mind, I'll tell them I broke it.

I'll give the bottle to Eytan. I trust him: he won't tell anyone. And he'll do what I ask: he'll throw the bottle into the sea, in your country, in Gaza.

Of course if Efrat knew all this she'd say that a message in a bottle isn't much of a means of communication in a modern world, that I'm behaving like a character in a film. And I'd say that's exactly what I want to do, make films. But I've got this idea that, to make films, you have to have a good grasp of reality first.

I don't know whether the mail works well between us

17

and the Palestinian territories, whether there's any censor-
ship. So I'll give you an e-mail address I've set up just for
you to write to. It's bakbouk@writeme.com *

There, I hope you'll reply. It's a bit bland to say it, but it's
the truth: I really hope you will.

Yours,

Tal

Yesterday evening I went into Eytan's bedroom just before
he went back to his base. There was an impressive collec-
tion of stuff on his bed: socks, T-shirts, packets of cigarettes,
CDs, and his CD player. And his gun too, of course, which
I avoided looking at.

Just like every time he leaves, I could think only of the
dangers he was facing: not a month goes by without some of
our soldiers dying in Gaza. Mom always has trouble holding
back her tears, and he has trouble holding back his irritation.

"Come on, I *have* grown a bit since nursery school, you
know, Mom. I'm not a complete baby anymore," he tells
her, staring down from all of his six feet.

"I know, but I don't like you being over there."

"Well, you should have engineered a different future for
us."

Mom hates it when he says that. She doesn't like being
held directly responsible for the Middle East situation. But,
as she doesn't want to argue with her big boy of twenty,
just before he goes away (and what if he never came back?),

Bakbouk means "bottle" in modern Hebrew.

she doesn't say anything, kisses him, gives him money, and asks whether he's remembered his cell phone charger.

My big brother smiled at me. "Have you come to give me last-minute advice too?"

"Eytan, there's something I want to ask you," I said, holding the wrapped bottle in my arms.

"Are you playing with dolls again?" he said with a mocking grin.

"I'd like to remind you that I've *never* played with dolls because you told me dolls woke up in the night and bit people's toes and turned their bedrooms upside down."

"And you believed me?" he asked, amazed.

"Obviously! But listen, this is really serious," I went on. "In this package there's a bottle. I want you to throw it into the sea, in Gaza."

That wiped the smile off his face.

"Are you crazy, Tal? I'm not allowed to throw anything anywhere, especially over there! If someone sees me, there could be an inquiry; I might be arrested. You don't seem to realize: Gaza's like a powder keg. Strike a match and the whole place goes up. You'll have to tell me what's in this bottle, at least, and why you want me to throw it in the sea."

"No, I can't tell you. Well, I don't want to tell you. But I promise you it isn't drugs or weapons or any kind of contraband."

He thought for a moment, frowning.

"You're sure this isn't going to turn into a stupid mistake?" he asked.

"Positive. Please do it. You're the only person I can ask."

He took the package and stuffed it in the middle of the pile of T-shirts.

"Okay," he said with a sigh, "but you are weird . . ."

I kissed him on both cheeks. Very hard.

Now all I can do is wait. And hope Eytan doesn't get into trouble because of me.

And keep my fingers crossed for something to happen, of course.

Something wonderful.

The Reply

From: Gazaman@post.com
To: bakbouk@writeme.com
Subject: (no subject)

Hi,

I warn you from the start I haven't got long dark hair or hazel eyes—and plucked eyebrows too, maybe?—and all that drivel which went on for half your letter. I'm more along the lines of a black mustache and very hairy legs. Well, I'm joking about the mustache, I shaved it off a few years ago, because of people from your country in fact . . .

I had a good laugh reading your letter! I nearly injured myself. You should get into comedy—you've got quite a career ahead of you, especially over here!

Miss Bottle-Full-of-Hope-in-a-Sea-of-Hatred, I have to inform you that I'm a boy. Oh yes, when you throw a bottle into the sea you have to be prepared for all eventualities, including not getting to your dream addressee. Anyway, if it had been a girl who found your bottle she would probably have used it as a candlestick and not been able to read the beautiful prose from this pure, sensitive daddy's girl. Palestinians can't read Hebrew, my dear, at least not in Gaza. Surely you don't think they teach us the *language of the enemy*, with big tests at the end of every term, working toward exams, studying *your* authors? Or maybe you think Palestinian children get thrashed by their parents for having bad grades in Hebrew! I can read your letter and write to you and even bother to take any interest in you because I had to learn Hebrew, and I even—

I don't feel like explaining. I'm replying because you entertained me for a bit with your stories—you don't write too badly. But the rest of it, holding out a hand to the nasty Palestinians who may not be as nasty as all that, how much you like films, your father, your teachers, your best friend, all that: I don't give a damn!

And even then I'm being polite . . .

Sign up for a film course, or send your letter to a competition for something like Children for Peace. I'm sure UNESCO organizes loads of things along those lines with children's drawings full of injured doves looking like half-dead chickens and olive branches strewn all over the ground and acrostic poems of the word "peace." (Yes, acrostic poems! Can you believe it, in Gaza they cram children's heads full of words they'll only use in literature lessons too! We're practically the same, the two of us, indeed!)

My little cousin entered a competition like that and he was really happy when they sent him a box of chocolates. Except that the organization that gave them to him had bought the chocolates in Israel and his father threw them away. "We don't eat enemy chocolates," he told Yacine. And of course Yacine cried and said they were the "chocolates of peace" and that he had worked hard writing his poem without a single mistake, and coloring the dove's blood without going outside the lines, but his father wouldn't give in. He's a hard man, my uncle Ahmed.

Right, I'm not going to tell you my life story. It's what you want, but I don't. I'm not some monkey you can watch to see how closely I resemble a human. You've got your biology teacher for that.

Good-bye forever!

Me

P.S. Your bottle wasn't in the sea, just buried into the sand a bit. Your brother must have a better grasp of reality than you.

P.P.S. "Gazaman" is a lot better than "bakbouk." Doesn't it bother you being called "bottle"? Maybe you're that sort of shape . . .

From: bakbouk@writeme.com
To: Gazaman@post.com
Subject: Please . . .

Dear Gazaman,

I've checked my mailbox ten times a day for the last two weeks and not found anything, so when I saw I had a new message today my heart started thumping really hard. You write well too, you know. And I'm not making fun of you when I say that. You act as if you couldn't give a damn about anything, including me, but I don't think you really mean it.

23

I like the way you say things: while I was reading, I could see your cousin Yacine as if I knew him.

You answered my letter without really answering, of course. But you answered all the same. That's what matters to me.

I didn't like your bit about monkeys, but I understood it. It's not true, I don't want to watch you like some peculiar animal. But that's what you thought, or wanted to think, from my letter.

Please can we start at the beginning again: I'm a girl, you're a boy, we live sixty miles apart. I don't have any trouble imagining the life of an American girl who lives six thousand miles away. Well, it makes sense: I've got TV and satellite, and right now there must be at least five series about students in American colleges (my mother calls it a cultural transfusion). But I can't begin to imagine *your* life, Gazaman. And that doesn't make sense. We're separated by years of war, by bomb attacks here perpetrated by Palestinians and military operations in your country carried out by our army. I know that sometimes they close your borders, that you're not allowed to travel, that poverty has gotten worse with the intifada. I also know that there are people where you live who dance in the streets when they hear that innocent people have been killed here. Of course that hurts but the real point is I just don't understand how people can jump for joy when they hear that babies, young children, ordinary men and women, or old people have died, simply because they were Israeli, and because they were in the wrong place at the wrong time.

But none of that tells me what your life is like. I think—probably naively, almost definitely naively in your eyes—that if people like you and me try to get to know each other, the future might have a chance of turning out some other color than the red of spilled blood and the black of hate.

You could have thrown my bottle away, or used it as a candlestick, like you said. But you replied and I'm clinging to that thought. Please give me (give us) a chance.

Yours,

Tal

P.S. To be honest, I've never received a letter I found as interesting as yours. I'd really like to hear from you again. That's all.

From: bakbouk@writeme.com
To: Gazaman@post.com
Subject: Stubborn

Dear Gazaman,

I'm stubborn. You're stubborn. We're stubborn.

You by staying silent.

Me by wanting to write to you.

Us . . .

Of course that "us" doesn't mean anything. But it could have some meaning if you weren't playing hide and seek with me. You replied to me once—you can't behave as if we haven't said anything to each other.

The two of us don't have much luck: we were born in the twentieth century—the bloodiest century in history, as Rosebush reminded us yet again yesterday. Two world wars, the Soviet empire dominating part of the world + conflicts pretty much all over the place with increasingly sophisticated weapons = hundreds of millions of deaths. "It's just math," he added with an almost sadistic smile. We felt very depressed after his lesson. Shlomi, our class representative, said history lessons should be banned, especially in times of conflict, because they sap morale too much. Mrs. Feldman (the biology teacher, in case you'd forgotten) comforted us by saying it was also the century of antibiotics and vaccines, which meant millions of lives saved. If you really think about it, that certainly balances out the deaths from the two wars. After her lesson we had computers with Sam, Olympic medalist of teachers. (He's young. He's gorgeous. He's got eyes as blue as the skies over Jerusalem at six o'clock in the morning. He's funny.) Shlomi asked him what he thought of the twentieth century.

"A lot of bad, of course. But it's the century when we, the Israelis, had a country, a flag, a national anthem. And computers were invented and that's good news for me personally; otherwise I'd certainly be unemployed right now."

So you see, what with wars, deaths, antibiotics, and

computers, the twentieth century was pretty busy. But what about the twenty-first, Gazaman? What are you doing with it? The future, your people, mine, our war, don't you think the two of us could talk about it?

If you like you can carry on hiding behind your pseudo-nym, but not behind your address, which isn't replying.

Bye,

Tal

An Argument with Myself

She has sent me five e-mails and I haven't replied. The problem is I can't stop thinking about the girl. She deserves better than my sarcasm. And she's so sincere it knocks you out.

I found her bottle when I was walking by the sea. The beach is the only place where you can forget we're hemmed into this paltry corner of land called the Gaza Strip. No one who hasn't seen it can imagine the place. The easiest way to describe it is to list everything that isn't there, then I imagine you might have some idea of it: no rivers, no forests, no mountains, no valleys, no historical monuments, no spanking new shopping malls, no pretty streets with cafés and expensive shops, no big parks where families can go for picnics, no zoos. The Gaza Strip is just sand, a few olive trees, the shiny-bright enclaves where the Israeli settlers live, and gray houses, tens of thousands of gray houses huddled together, huddled so tight they nearly suffocate . . . and you do suffocate pretty easily here. Basically, it's the region's garbage dump. And who else lives here? One and a half million Palestinians dreaming of a Palestine; one and a half million Palestinians dreaming of a normal life (when they're not dreaming of killing an Israeli or, better still, ten of them, because hate and a thirst for revenge come cheap and are everywhere. In fact, they're the only commodities we have in plentiful supply, along with despair, that is).

I was sitting on the sand looking at the sea, envying the fish, which don't need permits to move to different waters. I thought about the dreams we had back in 1993, of the big hotels we wanted to build. My father had said, "You'll see, all the tourists will come to us, it's going to be better than Lebanon, we've got the most beautiful beach in the world. They will all travel through this place, we're en route between the pyramids in Egypt and Jerusalem. There won't be anywhere better than Gaza beach . . ." He could already picture the girls in their swimsuits on lounge chairs, a promenade planted with palm trees and bougainvillea, little cafés serving *leben*, carob juice, fig juice, and mint tea.

I liked listening to him, at first. It was a time when everyone was happy. We signed the Oslo agreement with the Israelis, Yasser Arafat was going to come to Gaza, the Israelis were going to leave, in five years tops we would have a country. No, we weren't happy, we were intoxicated, reeling from all those wonderful promises of peace. How many times have I heard that word: "peace"! until I was

29

first dizzy with it, then nauseated, and finally sick. My father, who carried on with his plans for transforming Gaza into a seaside resort (in his head, only in his head), gave me a permanent feeling of indigestion too.

That's what I was thinking about, scratching the sand with my left hand, letting it run through my fingers, rubbing my thumb and forefinger to feel every last grain. There are endless things you can do with sand.

I lay down.

I sat back up. Immediately. Something had jabbed me viciously in the back. I can remember it now: I felt as if some huge injustice had been done to me, that I'd been cruelly attacked just as I was trying to forget myself in the sand—reducing myself to a body, its imprint on the ground, leaving the nausea and indigestion to hover overhead and be carried away on the wind.

I hauled the stone out to throw it far out to sea, so that it could disintegrate and enjoy an interesting future as sand rather than a useless life as an unintentional weapon, but it turned out I had a bottle in my hand.

An Israeli bottle. I knew that right away; I can tell. A bottle with paper rolled up inside it. I thought that happened only on desert islands in adventure stories, but it happened to me, here, in Gaza.

I lay down on the sand again—and it was soft and welcoming this time—and I read.

Funny girl. Strange but quite touching idea. This Tal would definitely be worth investigating in different circumstances. That's what I thought at the time.

The things she said got to me, and that annoyed me. I hate feeling two things at once; it's like having an argument with myself.

I went to the nearest Internet café. I sent her a reply, making sure no one saw who I was writing to. If you have nonaggressive contact with Israelis in this place they pretty quickly think you're a collaborator. And that suspicion is equivalent to a death sentence. You step out of your front door one day and *bang!* before you know it you land face down on the concrete, everyone else can have the oxygen now, you won't be needing that, you're a goner. I know, it's really stupid, but that's war for you. This idiotic war in which Israelis kill Palestinians and Palestinians kill Israelis and, there you go, it starts all over again. Actually, who started it? Them? Us? You? Me? No one can remember. Short memory, memory lapse, amnesia, hypocrisy, deliberate bad faith. Okay, come on, let's start again just to see who can kill the most, who's the best: them with their fighter planes, their shells, their short accurate M-16s, or us with our cheap, not very technological human bombs churned out by Hamas and the Islamic Jihad, yes, that's right, the ones who pray to God five times a day, the ones with bumps on their foreheads because they bang them on the ground so often, the ones who look down their noses at girls who don't wear a burka, and who want the impossible, in other words to throw the Israelis out, into the sea. They dream of all Israelis dying, drowning, not a single Jew left on Arab soil, leaving us—the Palestinians of this liberated Palestine—to the sharia. Yup, obeying

Islamic law to the letter, not drinking alcohol, not eyeing girls, not listening to rap and techno, that stuff's for the unclean, for Westerners, for American devils, and anyone Americanized. We, the Muslims, are pure, so life has to be free of any self-interest, waiting patiently for death (if possible as a martyr, if possible taking a few evil Americans with you, or some Jews if you can find them) because afterward you don't have to worry, you'll be in paradise with all its wonders, your time on earth is nothing, a meaningless little episode that has to be filled by going to the mosque five times a day and rearing twelve children the rest of the time.

Is that really what life is?

Shit.

So there you are. I get angry very quickly if I think too much, but I don't want to stop thinking. My head is the only place where no Tsahal soldier, no guy from Hamas, and not even my father or my mother can get in. My head is my home, my only home, a bit small for everything I've got to put inside it, and that's why I started writing, several years ago now. I didn't have to wait for that spoiled little Tal from Jerusalem to get me started. I write and then I burn the paper, tear it up, soak it, and throw it down the toilet; I'm too frightened someone will find it. But at least it does me some good, it soothes me a bit. There are too many people I hate, too many people stopping me from living my life, and too many signs (which aren't actually there but I can see all over the place) that say: EVERYTHING IS BANNED.

Three Shots Fired on Kings of Israel Square

From: bakbouk@writeme.com
To: Gazaman@post.com
Subject: Sadness

Dear Gazaman,

I know, I can tell, you're reading these. You'll end up replying sooner or later, so I'll keep on writing; it does me good.

It's the fourth of November, exactly eight years since our prime minister Yitzhak Rabin's assassination. Yesterday evening, like every year, there was a big gathering in the square named after him in Tel Aviv. And, like every year, we went along, my father, my mother, and me. "It's a pilgrimage we can't miss," my father says. "It proves we have faith in his vision of peace." Aviv Geffen, who was every teenager's idol ten years ago, sang, and so did David Broza. He strummed away on his guitar, playing his perennial song "Yihiye Tov." Mom muttered, "He's been singing that same song for twenty years, saying everything's going to be fine, ever since the war with Lebanon. Does he really still believe it?"

The concert and the speeches were beautiful but sad. There was a minute's silence at the exact time when Rabin was assassinated. It gave me goose bumps. I remembered that fateful evening when it felt as if the sky fell and the ground slipped from under our feet, when we felt orphaned and lost.

I was nine. It was two years after the Oslo agreement, after that day when I saw my parents cry for joy. In the intervening time, you may remember this, we'd suffered the first suicide attacks. Nowadays no one's surprised by the idea of people killing others by taking their own lives, but at the time everyone kept asking: how can it be possible? How can a man feel his heart beating, how can he breathe, feel hot or cold, see the light of day, know that he is alive . . . and activate a mechanism to blow up his own body? Isn't he frightened? And how can he look at the people around him, men, women, and children, living people like himself, healthy people, thinking about their humdrum little lives, their worries, their loves, their children? Doesn't he feel any pity? Does he choose his victims?

Good-looking people rather than ugly ones, young rather than old?

I still ask myself these terrible questions, Gazaman, even if ten years later it has been decreed that that's the way it is, that it all boils down to hate and that's all there is to it.

I'm back on the subject of the fourth of November 1995. The left-wing and all movements in favor of peace decided to gather together in support of Yitzhak Rabin, to tell him that, even if some Israelis were against him and called him a traitor because he was negotiating with the Palestinians, there were others in the country who supported him, who wanted a solution, who longed for peace with two separate states: Israel and Palestine.

My parents never missed a single peace demonstration. They were even on that same square in Tel Aviv demonstrating for Israel to withdraw from Lebanon the day I was born! Mom had contractions halfway through a David Broza song (him again); she was rushed to the hospital, and that's why I was born in Tel Aviv when all of my mother's family had been born in Jerusalem for four generations. "And you were born under the sign of our fight for peace," my father always says. "That's a comfort."

So then, on that fourth of November, on that square that was then known as Kings of Israel Square, we arrived so early—my parents, Eytan, and me—

that we were in the front row. Eytan and I had made a sign: WE'RE WITH YOU, RABIN. We'd argued over who would write the big blue letters on the sign. Mom had interrupted, saying we should both write them. I made a spelling mistake in "with you," but we were in a hurry and didn't have time to start again, so Dad said it didn't matter, that spelling mistakes were quite touching—they showed that even children took an interest in what was happening in the country. And they actually showed us on TV— my grandparents saw us and said we were very telegenic.

It was a really fun evening, our favorite singers were there, there were at least a hundred and fifty thousand people, my parents bumped into tons of friends, it was a party. At the end they all sang the "Song for Peace" up on the stage. Even Rabin sang. I saw him from close up; he was quite red, a bit like me when I have to go up to the blackboard, and he sang out of tune. I laughed because it was so funny seeing the prime minister singing—especially out of tune—but Mom said it wasn't polite, that he was doing his best and we shouldn't make fun of people who mean well.

We went to a café with some friends of my parents. There were lots of children still singing, and older people too. I can remember thinking I loved demonstrations, that it would be good if we could have one every week.

Then the café owner suddenly turned up the volume on the radio. That happens a lot here, as soon as something serious happens.

Within a few seconds everyone was silent, apart from a baby crying.

A news flash: "A man fired at Prime Minister Yitzhak Rabin this evening, a few minutes after he came off the stage where he had been singing the 'Song for Peace' with thousands of people gathered in Tel Aviv. He is in critical condition in Yichilov Hospital. In a moment we will be going live to our correspondent outside the hospital."

Stunned silence. Devastated faces. Consternation.

Then all the adults' faces distorted, like in a horror film. It looked as if their cheeks, foreheads, and chins were turning to liquid and the liquid was dissolving into something invisible. Their eyes were lakes of fear. They bit their own fingers and moaned.

They cried out. They howled. They burst into tears. All of them. Including my parents, who fell into each other's arms. And, with a slight delay, the children started sobbing too, not really understanding because everything had happened too quickly, but it was terrifying enough seeing that crowd that had been so happy suddenly transformed into a huge wail of despair.

You have to have lived through that to understand it, Gazaman. You have to have seen it and heard it.

I remember it all, in minute detail. When I think back

to it, I know it was that moment that made me want to make films. I can't say why.

We stayed at the café a long time. The journalist was still talking on the radio but he wasn't telling us anything; he couldn't tell us anything, because he himself knew nothing. He kept saying that someone had shot Prime Minister Yitzhak Rabin and that he would soon be talking to the spokesperson at Yichilov Hospital.

Someone shouted, "Those Palestinian bastards! They'll pay for this!"

Mom and Dad told me that everyone thought a Palestinian had killed our prime minister. No one could imagine any other scenario.

But . . . an hour later, I think, the journalist had given another news flash. Yitzhak Rabin was dead. Assassinated by a student. An Israeli Jew.

The crying started again. Mom said, "This is the end of the world. The beginning of the apocalypse."

The café owner didn't want anyone to pay. He said it was an evening of mourning and that he didn't want to make money that night.

We went back to the square. Thousands of people had had the same idea. They walked about aimlessly, stopped, hugged, wept. A shopkeeper brought out his entire stock of candles. We lit them and sat around them; some young people sang sad songs in soft, hushed voices.

That was eight years ago, Gazaman. And yesterday evening I cried all over again, like I do every year when we go there to remember him.

And I thought of you.

Tal

And the Brakes Were Slammed On . . .

From: Gazaman@post.com
To: bakbouk@writeme.com
Subject: Yeah, right . . .

Hi, your majesty,

Don't start shouting triumphantly and dancing around the room like girls do when they're happy. I'm writing to you but that doesn't mean we're friends, okay? We haven't tended sheep together is an understatement. You've sent me six e-mails. I'm polite, I'm answering, that's all.

Well, it's also that your e-mail about Rabin's assassination stirred things up a bit. I wasn't in the front row of the stalls like you and your family, but I remember it perfectly.

You weren't expecting that, were you? That it had quite an effect on us too, that whole business. But let your little head have a good think about it: there was this man, an Israeli, who first saw the light of day twenty-five years after our land was occupied, forty-five years after the war that gave you a country. He thought to himself, "Hang on, those poor people living in refugee camps and shabby villages, they really do exist, they might even be human beings." And he made up his mind that he would get you to accept the idea, to give us a little something, a hint of autonomy, a scrap of independence.

I'm not saying that everyone here was over the moon—there's no pleasing some people, they want everything and then more, but that's another story.

Still, me and my family and other people we know were seriously pleased. We thought: we're going to have a normal life at last. Our own police (and not your terrible soldiers!), traffic lights that work, homegrown film stars, a national football team, compulsory military service, schools open to everyone all day long . . . (Actually, to be honest, that was the downside of the whole thing: because there aren't enough school buildings, children go to school either in the morning or the afternoon. So a bit of normality wasn't great for anyone who hates sitting in front of a blackboard all day. But, as you can imagine, no one was really bothered about that in Oslo or Washington or the press; they were hardly going to stop the whole peace process for a few whining idiots.)

Then Rabin was assassinated. I heard a neighbor shout it out of her window. Her voice sounded strange and shrill, shaky. I burst out laughing because you really couldn't tell whether she was shrieking with joy or crying.

My father shot me a furious look. He said, "Shit, shit, shit, this is bad news for us," and he switched on the TV.

Do you know what? At first we thought it was us who bumped

41

him off too. Well, a Palestinian, I mean. It was logical. Hamas or Jihad had decided it was time the brakes were slammed on the peace process and the best way to do it was to take out the train driver. We flipped. Killing a prime minister, even the Israeli one, was serious stuff. It would come back to haunt us. But how?

And then afterward they said he was a Jew, the assassin. An Israeli. Well, we just couldn't believe it. They could have told me the next Star Wars film was going to be made in Gaza with Arafat as Anakin Skywalker and I would have found it more credible. Some people took several hours to process the information, others had this quiet little smile. So, they're killing each other now. Well, why not? Means we don't have to do the dirty work.

Mind you, we very soon realized that it was really bad news for us. I think the Israeli government even decided to seal off the Gaza Strip. Do you know what that means or shall I draw a picture? Okay, I'll draw a picture, with words, because I can't draw on e-mail.

Here's the Gaza Strip. Fifteen miles long, six wide. All around the outside, barbed wire with seven "crossing points." If something slightly violent happens here or anywhere else or on the Israeli side of the moon, if the Israelis are worried we're going to blow them up, then *bang!* they close the crossing points. It's like a faucet. You turn it, squeeze it tight, there's no more water. Afterward everyone feels a bit more relaxed. The Palestinians are hermetically sealed, stewing in their own juice, pickles in a jar, if you like.

Basically, we hadn't done anything but we ended up shut in anyway. Like a little boy who's been smacked. "But I didn't do anything, Daddy!" "Shut up and go to your room, otherwise I'll smack you again and you'll know why!"

So there you are. Rabin was dead, the train had been stopped, and we were stuck at the station, not knowing whether there were any more trains scheduled. Completely up the creek.

You try living with something like that, Miss Morning Dew (I'm good at Hebrew, aren't I? I even know what your name means). You try living with the thought that, whatever goes on around here, it always comes right back in our faces.

Do you think that's fair?

Bye,

Gazaman

From: bakbouk@writeme.com
To: Gazaman@post.com
Subject: WANTED

Name: unknown

Age: unknown

Marital status: unknown

Father's name: unknown

Mother's name: unknown

Number of brothers and sisters: unknown

Favorite pastime: making fun of others?

Place of residence: Gaza

Pseudonym: Gazaman

Distinguishing features: claims to be polite but says, "Hi, your majesty." Has a sense of humor, I would even say Jewish humor. A liking for secrecy too.

Thank you for your description of Rabin's assassination as seen by the Palestinians. It was vivid, you could say, interesting, with a clear eye for descriptive detail. But you're under no obligation to pull me to pieces systematically; it's ridiculous. I do have something between my ears, if you can believe it, and if I have to ladle on the irony every five lines to prove it to you, I will get down to it right away. You may not know this but we are the champions of classic humor, dark humor, irony, and the ultimate put-down. A people that has suffered for two thousand years inevitably builds up ammunition against despair.

If you really are polite, introduce yourself for goodness' sake.

And, in answer to your question: no, it's not fair that everything comes right back in your faces.

Haven't got time to say more about it today. I've got an English test tomorrow, and I won't improve my chances in that by writing to you.

Bye,

Tal

From: Gazaman@post.com
To: bakbouk@writeme.com
Subject: Match results

Okay. You've scored, let's say, half a point. The little e-mail with my statistics—like an information sheet for teachers at the beginning of the year, or for the secret service, that wasn't a bad idea. You've still got quite a way to go. Hang in there, don't wear yourself out. I'm sure a nice daddy's girl like you goes Rollerblading and plays tennis, with a pretty headband in her hair. You can add jogging, for endurance—it will increase your chances of improving your score.

But you'll have to wait a bit for the answers. I've got to go now.

And I'm not telling you where.

I can be very busy too.

Seriously.

Fighting Boredom

From: bakbouk@writeme.com
To: Gazaman@post.com
Subject: It's too quiet

Hello, Gazaman,

Winter's here.

It's cold.

The days feel like short little interruptions to the night.

I went to the cinema with Ori yesterday to see *The Return of the King*. We had an argument on the way home. About nothing. For the first time.

I think it started when I said Orlando Bloom was quite attractive even though he's not my type.

He latched on to the "quite attractive" and just went ballistic.

It's incredible how one little sentence can unleash so many others. He started by accusing girls in general ("You're all so superficial, you're only interested in good-looking men. What about the ugly ones, don't they have a right to exist?" etc.) then accusing me in particular of loving him less than before and seeing less of him.

I didn't know what to do, I kept saying, "No, no, that's not true." He walked me home, didn't kiss me, and left.

It's Saturday today. No school, everything's closed, the whole place feels dead. My brother, Eytan, hasn't had any leave; he's still over your way, in Gaza. Funny, isn't it? Well, "funny" probably isn't the right word, but that's what we say when something's strange. I often think that you could see my brother one day, but you wouldn't know it was him, and he wouldn't know it was you.

I feel all empty. I've called Ori several times on his cell. It rings, then I get his voicemail. He's obviously screening his calls. I don't like that.

I'm bored, I'm so bored . . . What do you do when that happens?

Send me an answer.

Tal

From: Gazaman@post.com
To: bakbouk@writeme.com
Subject: Thinking straight

If you want my opinion, Ori thinks you're soft in the head

and he's had enough but doesn't know how to tell you so he finds any excuse to let you know. Or he's in love with another girl but would rather it was you who left him, and the best way of going about that is to have as many arguments with you as possible.

Apart from that, it doesn't say THERAPIST across my forehead. What exactly makes a relationship work between a boy and a girl? Where's the boundary between just sex and proper love with beating hearts and eyes full of tears for the one person they just can't live without? I don't know, I DON'T KNOW! Please don't talk to me about your love life anymore.

I prefer your other subject for today's dissertation: "What do you do when you're bored?" the little girl asked the big bad wolf in her gentle voice. And this is what the big bad wolf replied:

In Gaza you can't help being bored. Unless you're an old man with loads of memories to tell others about, or a mother with meals to prepare, washing to do, and children to dress. Or a girl who helps her mother do all that. Or a man of thirty-five or over who is allowed to work in Israel because, statistically, the guys who blow themselves up are under thirty-five, so that whole age group—the glorious youth, as they might say—isn't allowed to work there. Or if you're very devout and get up at four in the morning to go to the first prayers, praying five times a day. (Can you imagine that?) When you talk to God five times a day, you don't notice time passing . . .

When you're none of the above, when you're me, you're condemned to boredom. And, to avoid dying of boredom, you look for every possible way of wringing the neck of this peculiar beast that's got you in a stranglehold and makes you wander around in circles saying, "I dunno what to do, there's nothing to do, what the hell can I do?"

Solution number one: you play cowboys and Indians for real (if you live in a refugee camp). You go out with a few friends and throw stones at Israeli soldiers. You're the good guys, they're the bad guys; it's simple. If it's your lucky day there could be a foreign cameraman around; he might film you hurling your stones and your hatred, and you'll be the star on the world's screens that evening. You take off your T-shirt to show your muscles, isn't life wonderful, you're no longer sure whether you're in a film or in your own reality . . . and does it really matter? You're enjoying yourself, running with the others, throwing stones, running some more, hiding with a hint of fear, a tiny hint of fear in your stomach, but not quite the fear of being killed (yet), only of being caught—just like hide-and-seek, isn't it? And sometimes one of your friends is injured. He steals the limelight from you because the cameraman has spotted him and zooms in on him, the ambulance comes with its siren wailing, everyone turns their attention to the hospital, the doctors whine because they can't work in these conditions, with all these kids milling around them while they're trying to assess whether the victim is slightly, seriously, or fatally injured. They say "go on, get out, go and play somewhere else," and you and your friends don't really know what to do so you shout, you demonstrate your anger in front of the foreign cameraman who's still there, because he was herded back too when he went in to film the victim up close. I mean, they couldn't exactly let him into the operating room, could they?

That's the first option, the most commonly accepted, the

one you see on TV and that you very probably believe in, the one which makes all the boys in Palestine look like brothers, interchangeable. Was one of them killed? No problem, there are three hundred thousand understudies, three hundred thousand bit-part actors who'd love to have the role. And I can't cope with those images any longer; they make me feel sick. What the hell is that game they've been broadcasting live on TV for the last fifteen years, going on and on but never ending? What does that caricature mean? We even started believing it ourselves, believing that was all we were: kids throwing stones at the evil soldiers to try and drive them away. The singular doesn't exist anymore: no me, you, him, her, there's just the plural—Palestinians. The poor Palestinians. Or the evil Palestinians, it all depends. But the plural is always there. To anyone who loves us without knowing us or who loathes us without knowing us, we're never one + one + one, but the whole four million. We all carry our whole people on our backs and it's so, so heavy, it's crushing, it just makes you want to close your eyes.

I'm calming down. I'm trying to calm down. First of all, it's not true that it's always boring here. There are Internet cafés (mind you, only for those who can afford them) but they're almost always full, full of young people who think they're magic: you just click and you're somewhere else, you're master of the world, you have everything—foreign music, football players, pretty girls with smooth hair wearing swimsuits and smiling at you. Then there are the games (strategy, lateral thinking, or combat), the sun setting over Sydney, catalogs of libraries from all over the world, films that have just been released in the States, people talking about their lives on personal sites (the first time they made love, their first heartbreak, childbirth), the weather in Bombay . . . and sites for very expensive schools, beautiful universities, societies for the protection of snails, organizations against smoking, in favor of smoking, in favor of the widespread introduction of scooters (including a demonstration of a proto- type for retired people and another with an integral baby carrier), and there are perfumes, cars, clothes, and porn sites, obviously, the Swiss television news, chat rooms with amusing pseudonyms, chat rooms with idiotic pseudonyms, in fact all the stupidity and incredible variety of the world right there, on the Web.

And there's TV, of course. Egyptian films with ridiculous love stories, nonstop news on Al Jazeera. And also, recently, a pro- gram on Lebanese TV that everyone was addicted to. They get a group of young people who want to be singers and put them in a house together. The public votes to eliminate the ones they don't like, and in the end there's a winner who has the right, the huge privilege, the incredible opportunity of recording their own album. No one here missed a single episode but the Islamists made a fuss, saying it was impure and decadent, that it wasn't a good example to set for young Muslims, and the program was taken off the air. I thought there was going to be a big uprising among young Arabs but it didn't happen; everyone kept their heads down. And some people secretly resorted to watching your program, *Kohav nolad*, which is along the same lines but I don't know who copied who. Obviously, it's less appealing because it's in

Hebrew and it's young enemy talent singing, but everyone here is very happy that the Israeli Arab is still in the competition, and we hope he's going to win.

A victory over you, without a single shot fired—can you imagine!

Bye,

G

Virtual Friend?

From: bakbouk@writeme.com
To: Gazaman@post.com
Subject: All right, you're the best!

Hi, Gazaman,

Yes, yes, you're the best, you're definitely the best! The best at annoying me, talking complete drivel about Ori, allegedly putting yourself in his shoes just because you're a boy, and crushing me with your nastiness just because I'm a girl. Luckily he and I made up before I got your e-mail. He told me he was really sorry, that he was tired because he'd been up late studying for his exams. He also said he thought I was a bit distant at the moment and he'd talked to his sister about it. She told him he was paranoid and that my love was so strong it'd contribute to global warming by melting the ice caps.

I adore Shira, Ori's sister. I'm sure you'd get on well with her. She's very funny, very intelligent, full of energy, and pretty, if you like girls who look like Jennifer Aniston. (You do know who that is, at least? She's in *Friends*.) She was the one (Shira, not Jennifer Aniston) who taught me how to say really banal things in a distraught, melodramatic way. It sounds stupid when I describe it like that, but it feels fantastic. You have to practice quite a lot. For example, if you get a bad grade in math, instead of just being annoyed or disappointed or dreading telling your parents, you have to keep sighing in despair and moaning, "Oh no! This can't be possible! It's horrific! I'm going to fail the whole term, the whole year, my exams! I'll never go to college, I'll beg on the streets but no one will ever give me anything, they'll tell me I'm young and I can work, I've got two arms and two legs, but no one will take me on, and if I don't have a job I won't have a family, no children, my life's ruined!" Afterward you remember that you said all that just because you failed a math test and it makes you laugh, you realize that it's such a minor upset, and a whole life can't be ruined by something like that. So that's Shira. I should add that she's studying drama in Tel Aviv, that she's fantastic at acting, and that if I ever make a film she'll get the lead role.

Back to you. You are weird, talking about love, or rather asking me not to talk about it. Have you ever been in love? Are you in love at the moment? I know you won't answer that, obviously. Gazaman, you really are the champion of secrets.

It's so funny that you know *Kohav nolad*! Did you know that the streets here are empty on Wednesday evenings when it's on? And don't worry about the Arab contestant—I bet he'll win. So, you see, everyone says we're racist and we don't like Arabs, but if an Arab wins the final of a singing competition that must mean there's still some hope for us all, don't you think?

I'm in a good mood today. Relaxed and happy because Jerusalem's been calmer recently, because my brother's got some leave and we're going to Tel Aviv together to party, because my boyfriend's not angry, and because I feel as if you and I are becoming friends a bit.

Well, "friends" might not be the right word; I'll have to find another one. "Virtual friends"?

Speak to you soon.

Love,

Tal

From: Gazaman@post.com
To: bakbouk@writeme.com
Subject: (no subject)

I don't know Jennifer Aniston; no one's thought of introducing us until today.

Neither do I have any desire to meet your boyfriend's sister.

I couldn't give a damn if an Israeli Arab wins some stupid singing competition. It won't change the fact that we don't have a country, a normal life, or the right to go where we want, when we want. And is a singer (and a bad one at that, if you want my opinion) really going to solve the whole Middle East problem? You really can be stupid sometimes! Most of the time even. There are some people who see evil in everything; you see hope in everything: on TV, in a bottle, perhaps even in the trash can. You could look at a black sky and say, "Oh, look at that lovely pink sky!" You could look at a field of thorns and ferret through it to find a flower. "Oh! Look, a little flower! That's a sign of hope!" I'm convinced that you'd even be able to recognize the word "hope" in a Japanese film with Korean subtitles. You're obsessed with it! It's an illness, you know.

You're happy—well, good for you. But I'm not your virtual friend.

And I can't see the point of *pretending* to be devastated by a bad grade in math. Really stupid idea. I can tell you, here no one has to pretend to be devastated; you really are all the time. And we have every reason in the world to be. I could make you a long list, a very long list, of all the reasons. But, if it's all right with you, I've got more important things to do.

G

From: bakbouk@writeme.com
To: Gazaman@post.com
Subject: I'm so sorry

You're angry again, or hurt maybe, and, once again, very hard on me. I don't know how to write to you anymore, what I should say and what I shouldn't. And I'm a bit fed up with it because you look down on me the whole time with no good reason, as if I were some little idiot who doesn't understand anything in life. And I'm sick to death of you always going on about how we're responsible for all *your* hardships! You know that my parents and me, all my family, have always been in favor of your having a state, for peace not to be just a word in songs, dictionaries, and speeches, but also a reality. So you can't accuse me of being against you or your people. And there's one question you never ask yourself: where exactly are *your* advocates for peace? Why are there never a hundred thousand Palestinians gathered together calling for peace with us, without hatred in their eyes? Why did the intifada break out three years ago when we, the Israelis, were prepared to give you a state? How can you accept the fact that terrorists kill women, children, babies? (I know, you're going to say that our army does the same thing, but there are people on this end who protest about it!) Why does no one on your end ever rebel against it or try to stop it happening? Do you know what my father said once? "I understand armed warfare between soldiers; I can even accept it. But not attacks on civilians." And his eldest son, my brother, is in Gaza, and my father knows he could be told he's dead at any time!

Do you ever think that we're not living in normal circumstances either? That it's not normal for parents to shake like a leaf when their children get on a bus or go to a café? Do you know that Efrat's parents have banned her and her sister from going out together in the evening? That way, if there's a bombing somewhere, they'll only lose one daughter and not both! Do you think it's normal for parents to think like that? Do you know that at my school there are three girls and two boys who've been injured in bombings, who are missing an arm or a leg or are horribly scarred?

So I'm really sorry if I've offended you without meaning to. I apologize. I don't have any problem saying I'm sorry. But it's as if every time I get a bit closer to you in my e-mails, every time some sort of friendship might develop between us, you put on your armor, bring out your arrows, and aim them at me.

As you so rightly said at one point: do you think that's fair?

Tal

From: bakbouk@writeme.com
To: Gazaman@post.com
Subject: Still angry?

Okay, you're not answering and in the meantime I've calmed down. I've read back through all your messages from the beginning: they confirm that you're unusual, complicated, and you mix up humor and anger. If you were, say, Australian and I were Norwegian, we could write to each other without ever getting angry—there's been no conflict between Australia and Norway to date, as far as I know. But maybe they've got a bit less to say to one another . . .

Either way, there are three things I'm sure of:

1) I'm not going to leave you alone until you answer.

2) I'm sure you've got a real secret.

3) You like me. Yes, you like me. Or you like writing to me and hearing from me, which is more or less the same thing.

Peace be with you, as we say in Hebrew, and as you do in Arabic.

Tal

Tal

What a strange game. Who's the cat and who's the mouse? We've been writing to each other for more than two months and I still don't really know what he's thinking. Mind you, it's no clearer this end. I didn't meet him in a chat room discussing something we're both interested in—films, music, some TV program . . . I just took it into my head to write to a Palestinian girl the same age as me and I landed up with a boy who won't say how old he is, a sort of flickering pen pal who switches on and off when he likes.

There are questions banging away inside my head like a door slamming in the wind. It's obsessive. What do I want from him? Friendship? Confrontation? To be disappointed? What do I want him to be for me? How do I want him to behave toward me? I've told him these questions wouldn't even need asking if I weren't Israeli and he Palestinian. But that's the way it is: we were born in a part of the world that's on fire, where people feel old very young, where it's almost a miracle if someone dies a natural death. And I want to go on believing that if he and I really managed to "talk" to each other, then it would prove that our nations aren't condemned to loathe one another for all time with no possible let-up.

For the first time in ages I've got a real secret. Something I haven't talked to Efrat or Ori about. When you've got a boyfriend and a best friend, you can always tell one of them the things you don't tell the other. But there it is, complete radio silence on the e-mails between Gazaman and Tal Levine. It's classified, top secret. Not that I really made the decision; it just happened. At the beginning I was worried they would stop me from giving the bottle to Eytan, they would think I was some sort of desperado and tell me it was dangerous or that someone would even ban me from exchanging e-mails with a boy from Gaza. In fact, there can't actually be a ban. I'm not the only one: peace campaigners are constantly in touch with the Palestinians, they even go into the territories. But I *could* be the only person having *this* sort of experience: an anonymous private contact. It's disconcerting. Who is it out there, really? E-mails are so easy, so deceptive. We're all unique, apparently, but one person can have ten different addresses—or a hundred, or a thousand—and a thousand pseudonyms. You can invent different identities and lie, and have discussions with other people who may be lying too. Everyone's safely hidden behind their computer screens, no one's taking any risks. You say what you think about things, talk about what you like and what you hate (colors, flowers, animals, singers, actors—does that actually say who you are?) but you don't get your feet wet; you're talking to a nobody, and they can't look you in the eye and see if you're lying or telling the truth. All you're looking at is your screen. A reflection. It's really irritating.

There, that's what I've been feeling the last few days: irritation. It's a nasty, sour feeling, it makes my throat rough and sore, and it feels like someone's pulling my head backward, not letting me go where I want to. I've formed a connection with a shadow and it's turning me into a bundle of nerves, making me laugh one minute and then hurting me the next, and I can't tell anyone about it. Ori's asked several times if there's something wrong. I said no. Efrat's a bit annoyed with me; she can't bear it if I hide anything from her and she's got a well-honed antenna for that sort of thing. She knows I've been lying to her about something ever since she saw me writing a letter in biology. Every time I catch her eye I can hear "beep, beep, beep—lie detected!" and I look away.

I feel as if this one tiny lie has woven a whole web around me. And I'm getting tangled up in the web and getting further and further away from everyone else. I can't seem to talk to them naturally. At the same time, I can't understand why I feel so uncomfortable: I've sent a few e-mails to some guy and he's replied when he felt like it. It's not as if I'm expected to publish a news bulletin every morning to keep all of Jerusalem up to date with the duration and content of my Internet connections. Still, there's something not quite right, and the others can feel it. I'd like to find the right acid to dissolve the tension. It would be so easy, magic, like a simple experiment in chemistry lab.

A bit later

I'm so lucky. Really very lucky. Dad didn't go to work today. He saw me go to the bathroom ten times to splash my face with cold water, he saw me take a couple of aspirin, and he didn't say, "Is something wrong, Tal? Have you got a headache?" That's the sort of sensible thing Mom would have said, but it wouldn't have actually meant very much, it wouldn't have opened any doors for me. You can usually just reply, "No, I'm fine," and go a bit further into your shell.

My dad knows when to speak and when not to. He also knows exactly what to say—with just a few words he can set everything straight when the neurons inside my brain are jumping in every direction.

He knocked on my door and waited for me to ask him in.

He looked me right in the eye with those green eyes of his and that smile that forms little creases up by his temples.

"Am I disturbing you, Tal?"

I shook my head and closed the book I was writing in— this book, in fact. If he noticed, he didn't show it.

"I know you're very busy and you've got your exams at the end of the year. And then there's Ori and your friends . . . But I wanted to ask you a favor. A favor you might find very interesting, actually . . ."

"Yes?"

"Right. There's an English television station that wants to make a documentary about Jerusalem. I've been asked to research some locations before they start filming. They want to bring out all the different aspects of the city and its inhabitants. Nothing revolutionary, I wouldn't think, the sort of thing that's been done a hundred times before—they just give it a new title. A few images of the Western Wall, the souk, Meah Shearim, Orthodox Jews dressed in black, Muslims in jellabas smoking hookahs, a handful of youngsters in a nightclub or at a café on Ben Yehuda Street, soldiers drinking orange juice with their rifles slung over their shoulders, and a final shot with the sun setting over the Old Town . . . The people who've gotten in touch with me don't want a montage of postcard pictures. What they want to do, like so many others before them, is to show a *different* Jerusalem, the *real* Jerusalem. I told them that was as difficult as writing a truly beautiful love story: there have already been so many attempts! And it's so difficult to capture! And then I thought of you . . . and I agreed to do it."

"*You thought of me!* I can't see the connection with the documentary, Dad."

"You're young. You're new. You happen to have been born in Tel Aviv but Jerusalem's your city. You see it and experience it as someone who'll spend the better part of their life in the third millennium. It's your point of view I need. I want to see the city through your eyes. If you agree to do it, I'll lend you my TV camera. You'll have to use it like a notepad, filming all the places that mean something to you, that tell the story of where you live, not where someone who's never set foot here *imagines* you live. I also happen to know you don't exactly hate using a camera . . ."

I threw my arms around his neck. (It's not something that happens every day now that I'm as tall as him, but this time I didn't even think.) I told him it would be fantastic, even if I wasn't sure I'd be up to it, because I've never done anything like it, and he was "Jerusalem's Sweetheart," a nickname Efrat gave him once when she was feeling particularly inspired. He told me he was only asking me because he knew I could do it and that he would take care of the more "traditional" locations.

"You'll be paid, of course," he added.

My eyes nearly popped out of my head.

"But surely I can't be paid for just wandering around my hometown, Dad? And with your camera too?"

"Of course you can. It's called work what you'll be doing. If you like it . . . well, so much the better, but first and foremost it's work."

"And when do your English people need my notepad?"

"In two months' time. Do I take that as a yes?"

"Yes, of course!"

"Thanks very much, Tal. You know where the camera is, I trust you to be careful with it."

And he left my room.

I thought how wonderful my father is: saying thank you when he knows full well he's the one doing me a favor! I can use his camera when I like! I can film more than just my cousin's wedding and Eytan going off to the army.

Apparently, I actually did quite a good job that day. I did close-ups of everyone's hands and most of the shots of Mom were from behind: she had tears in her eyes and it's not very kind filming someone crying . . . anyway, you might not think so, but backs communicate a lot.

Could my name be in the credits?

Could I make a lot of money?

I didn't dare ask. To be honest, it didn't even occur to me. (Not right away, anyway.)

From Jerusalem to Hollywood,
via Gaza

From: bakbouk@writeme.com
To: Gazaman@post.com
Subject: On the road to glory!

Dear Gazaman,

I've got some very good news to tell you: one of my dreams is coming true. Well, the beginnings of a dream, to be more precise, but you have to start somewhere. I'm going to work as an assistant on a film shoot. Okay, as Efrat pointed out, Orlando Bloom isn't in it, there won't be any famous actors in it because it's a documentary, but I'm going to have a camera in my hands, and my father's trusting me to find locations.

I'm so happy, and I just wanted to tell you.

Bye,

Tal

P.S. The documentary is about Jerusalem. I have to film the city as I see it, as I experience it. I'm going to ask you a very silly question: have you ever been to Jerusalem?

From: Gazaman@post.com
To: bakbouk@writeme.com
Subject: Re: On the road to glory!

Oh, I get it, you can already see yourself in Hollywood! You're not exactly lacking in confidence, are you? Don't expect me to jump for joy, though, or to send you a bunch of roses . . . Anyway, there aren't many florists around here . . .

I don't think I'm pleased for you. It's not like I'm a part of your wonderful project. No, I'm not pleased, but I'm jealous. And I'm going to write that again so that you know those words didn't just slip out: I'm jealous.

Bye,

Me

From: bakbouk@writeme.com
To: Gazaman@post.com
Subject: To clarify

I never said I could see myself in Hollywood, but when you've made up your mind to be like that there's no stopping you. It's been my dream for years: to be behind a camera, showing the things not everyone sees even when they're right before our eyes, telling a story. You should be able to understand that, shouldn't you? Don't tell me you don't have any dreams . . .

Okay, bye!

Tal

P.S. I feel I have to repeat everything with you: have you ever been to Jerusalem?

P.P.S. Actually . . . nothing. Or, no, this: can we agree that you're only nasty to me every other day, okay?

From: bakbouk@writeme.com
To: Gazaman@post.com
Subject: My first steps (and worried)

Dear Gazaman,

I'll start with why I'm worried: I haven't heard from you for a few days. I keep telling myself you're just like that, you write when you feel like it, say nothing when you feel like it, and I'll have to adapt. If you lived in (okay, I'm going to spin my globe and stick my finger on it at random) Italy or Canada, I'd think you were very busy, that you might have had a history test (if you were at school) or a relationship that was taking up all your time (if you were in love), a relationship that was getting you down (if you loved her very much and she didn't feel the same), a problem with your computer (if you had one at home), a bout of tonsillitis (if you still had your tonsils). The problem is, you're not a perfect representative of the conditional clause, you also happen to live in Gaza. (Where in Gaza, now that's another question. In

69

town? In a refugee camp?) They said on the news there was an operation being carried out in the Gaza Strip at the moment. Some Hamas activists have been killed— four, I think—but if I've got this right there were also some civilians who were killed or injured, according to the sources. I watched the images really closely, it was in the Khan Younes camp. I thought there was about a one in a million chance that you would appear in those images. But I've got no way of knowing. There were women pointing at a house completely destroyed by our soldiers, there were angry men, and children searching through the rubble for their things. It all seems so far away, I thought. Not far away like an inaccessible dream, but like a nightmare you're relieved not to be going through yourself. Yes, that's what I thought. A house that's been destroyed is a terribly sad thing; it must be hard not having much to your name and then suddenly to have nothing, to have to go and eat and sleep somewhere else. I even thought about how I would feel if my own house was destroyed and I felt all broken inside. I hoped you weren't in those pictures, that you weren't going through that.

Why? Why does it have to be like this? Why does my country—which I love, which is so beautiful, and where there are so many wonderful people—do that, over there, in your country? Because there are bomb- ings here, of course. Because we can't bear to see friends, neighbors, innocent people killed. But this really has to stop somewhere! I feel as if we're caught in a labyrinth and no one can find the way out, everyone's losing their temper and smashing everything in their efforts to get out into the fresh air.

I wanted to tell you about my first sessions in Jerusalem with my dad's camera. I went and filmed the Mahane Yehuda market. It was very bright and cheerful, the stallholders kept offering me fruit because (they thought) they were going to be famous thanks to me. But I've run out of time to write today. It doesn't matter, it can wait. Please just tell me if you're okay. And, be nice, no word games, no irony, nothing too cynical. Or maybe don't be nice. This time it wouldn't bother me at all. I'm sure that when you're cynical it's a sign that, deep down, you're not feeling too bad.

Bye then,

Tal

Gazaman

I'm trapped.

She caught me out.

And now I'm frightened.

I'm even frightened of writing the truth. What if a shell falls on me before I tear all this up? What if someone's spying on me or following me, because in this shitty little strip of land where everyone's always on top of everyone else, there's something suspect about anyone who wants to be on their own?

We're in the East, or in the Arab world, or in the Mediterranean. In all three cases, that means people think there's something wrong with you if you don't want to spend twenty-four hours a day with your family, your friends, and the other people at the mosque. Together. Always together.

But I think I'd end up going crazy if I could never be alone.

Her name is Tal. Tal Levine. She was born in Tel Aviv

on the first of July 1986, but she lives in Jerusalem, which she loves.

Her father is obviously pretty exceptional.

I've made as much fun of her as I could. I've enjoyed it. It's been a good way to relax. You can't really make fun of girls here—it's frowned on, even. Girls are respected, which means you don't look at them too much, you don't talk to them too much, and you marry them before doing anything interesting, even before kissing them.

I'm frightened of girls. And I don't feel like making fun of Tal anymore.

With girls, if they manage to get inside your heart, then you can't ever get them out, and it takes over completely, like a poison spreading through your whole body, you've had it, there's no antidote.

I know what I'm talking about.

I've never seen this Tal. And I probably never will. Ever. She's there without really being there. She's there on the screen at Aman Internet café. Her words on the screen, her energy, her questions. I always read it all very quickly, terrified someone might find out I'm in contact with an Israeli. An enemy, period. Satan dressed as a woman, which is worse than Satan as a man . . .

I change connection codes every day. I delete her messages as soon as I've read them. But I can't delete them from the hard drive in my head.

I can't believe it. In Jerusalem there's a seventeen-year-old girl, a Jew, an Israeli, who's thinking of me and of that ridiculous nickname, Gazaman. When I chose that pseudonym the main thing I wanted to communicate to her was that I was a man. That we're men. Even here, in Gaza. They—them over there—sometimes seem completely convinced that we're not.

But not her.

Her last message knocked me out. She described the destruction so well, much better than people who live here could have done. She had the right words, she put herself in our shoes, she could feel it all. And then there was that sentence: "Please just tell me if you're okay." I can still hear it, echoing endlessly. *Please just tell me if you're okay.*

I must be the only Palestinian in Gaza who's got someone worrying about them on the other side. UNESCO should have me classified as a historical monument or a world heritage site. They should film me and show me to the whole world as something rare and precious.

I've been caught in a trap by Tal Levine and it's terrible. It reminds me of something I swore I would never go through again. A girl inside my head. My heart beating hard.

No, no, no, I'm not in love with her. It's impossible, I've never seen her and she's bound to be very ugly, very fat, the sort who, the minute the temperature goes above seventy-five degrees, breaks into a sweat and gets big circles of sweat under her arms, yuk, it's disgusting. She's got a squint and the beginnings of a double chin, big ears that stick out, dark hairs on her upper lip, crooked teeth, eyes set too wide apart, eyebrows set too close together, and a hook nose. She's short with big feet and dirty hair she only washes every other Thursday; she walks like an elephant, talks like a bear with a heavy cold, looks like a depressed sheep, and thinks like a retarded sparrow, and there's plenty more where that came from.

No, no, no, of course not. I'm delirious, but I've had nothing stronger than water to drink and I haven't got a fever. She's bound to be pretty, or maybe even beautiful, but definitely pretty. Only complete idiots are really ugly. That's a rule I made up, but I do believe it. You can't be as sensitive, inquisitive, and intelligent as she is and have a face like a rat. People's qualities show on their faces, in their eyes, in whether or not they tense their lips when you're talking.

I promised myself, I swore to myself that I'd never fall into that trap again. With an Israeli girl, too. How could I be so unlucky! At one point she said, "I feel I have to repeat everything with you." But everything repeats itself. There was a First World War, then a Second. A first intifada, then a second. So for me, there was a first time, then . . .

No, no, no, this whole business is impossible because it's not logical and it can't really be happening. I couldn't really go and knock on Tal Levine's door, even if I had her address. I can't say, "Hi, it's me, I wanted to meet you for real, would you like to come and have coffee with me?" In real life there can only ever be me on one side and her on the other with our two nations loathing each other and firing at each other. We're the Romeo and Juliet of the third millennium, but there's no one to write our story.

I'm writing complete garbage. We're not Romeo and Juliet. She's got a boyfriend, she said that at the start, in the letter in the bottle, and she's mentioned him since. He's named Ori. It means "my light" in Hebrew. He must be a big jock type who does lots of push-ups because he's going off to his national service soon. She doesn't mention that, national service and the army, but in their country they all have to go when they're eighteen, so she and Ori will put on their smart khaki uniforms just like all the others. What would be really funny would be if he came here and I smashed his face in. What would be really absurd, really miraculous, and really terrible would be if she was the one who was sent to Gaza.

This really is garbage. I'm losing the plot. I should never have opened that bottle, I'd have been happier if it had been a bomb, if it had torn an arm off. I swore I'd never, ever . . .

As far as she's concerned, I'm not a friend, even if she tries to use nice words to describe me, but she does worry about me. It's enough to drive you crazy.

Her name is Tal. "Morning dew." It was another Tal who told me that.

Now I'd better tear all this up.

How a Name Can Be a Gift . . .

From: bakbouk@writeme.com
To: Gazaman@post.com
Subject: News, please!

I'm really worried now. They said on the radio that more people have been killed and injured in Gaza. I understand you not leaping to your computer to put my mind at rest, but I'd like some news of you. I've got a lump in my throat. Because, even if I still don't know much about you, Gazaman, I think I understand what's hiding behind the cynicism and the gibes. And I can't cope with this silence much longer.

Hoping to hear from you soon,

Tal

From: Gazaman@post.com
To: bakbouk@writeme.com
Subject: Re: News, please!

Hi, Tal,

No, I don't live in Khan Younes, and I'm not complaining about that; it's a pretty dismal place. But I know people who live there: they're very, very angry with you Israelis at the moment. If you're a believer you'd better pray your brother's not over there.

So, seeing as you're interested, I'm all in one piece and my neighborhood is peaceful. Yes, I said "neighborhood." Gaza isn't just a huge refugee camp, there are normal people here, living in normal apartments with a living room, two bedrooms, a bathroom and separate toilet, with a phone, a TV . . .

But there's been a curfew for several days and I couldn't get to the Internet café, or anywhere else for that matter. I hate whoever invented curfews. You can't imagine how awful it is, not being allowed to go out, for whatever reason. You're shut in, and no one cares if you're supposed to be going to see your grandfather or to do some shopping or to a hospital for treatment or even to have a baby.

Or if you want to go to the cinema, just to have something different to think about.

I'm tired. Tired of hearing ambulance sirens, angry crowds shouting, Hamas demonstrations calling everyone to join in the holy war, and airplanes and helicopters patrolling overhead. Tired of hearing radios and televisions on day and night, going on about the dead, the injured, homes that have been destroyed.

They say it's all America's fault, they're so powerful they could sort all this out if they really wanted to. They keep promising revenge. Terrible promises, terrible hatred. Tal, you can't imagine how tiring hate can be, how exhausting it is.

I often feel angry too. I keep thinking how my parents, my grandparents, and my great-grandparents were all born in Jaffa. They were happy there, life was good. Then the Jews came over from Europe and settled here. Why here? Because they were here a long time ago, they said. It was their native land. You know what happened after that, but you may not know all of it. You got your independence in 1948, no one in the region accepted it, and we went to war with you. My family was frightened of the fighting and left Jaffa. The Arab armies promised they would drive you out very quickly, promised we would soon be back home. Promises are wonderful things but we never went home. You won the war and we stayed stuck in Gaza, under Egyptian control. Ever since then something that you celebrate, your Independence Day, is a day of mourning for us, the Naqba, or "catastrophe." In 1967 there was another war, the Six-Day War. You won again. You conquered the territories we were living in and ever since then we dream of our own independence a bit more fiercely every day. And yes, I know, some people dream of your destruction. But not all. I don't think that's out of kindness, though. Do you think kindness has anything to do with politics? They couldn't care less, really, or they know only too well it would be impossible to destroy you.

My grandmother often told me about Jaffa and the house my family lived in. "It was a real palace," she used to say. "The net curtains would flutter in the cool breeze coming up from the sea.

The sea here is just as beautiful but there it seemed calmer, bigger, freer. In Gaza, my boy, even the sea feels like a prison to me." I liked listening to my grandmother talking. She had a gentle voice and lovely soft, tired eyes. She never got angry.

A few years ago I had a job in Israel (I might tell you about it one day). I went to Jaffa and looked for the house. When I found it, it was much smaller than I'd imagined, not as luxurious either. It wasn't a palace, just a simple stone house with a balcony in green forged iron. I took some pictures of it, making sure no one saw me. I could have been accused of spying . . .

When I gave the photos to my grandmother her eyes filled with tears. She hugged me and whispered, "You're not like other boys, Naïm. May Allah protect you till the end of your days. May He give you the strength to be who you are." She died shortly after that. We buried her with the pictures of the house.

There you are, Tal, that should have reassured you. I'm not dead. I'm not injured. I'm just very tired.

Bye,

Naïm (that's "paradise" in Arabic)

From: bakbouk@writeme.com
To: Gazaman@post.com
Subject: Thanks a million!
Attachment: Talgalil.jpg

Dear Naïm (a name at last, your name!),

I've read your e-mail over and over again, I know it by heart now. Reading about what you call being tired really moved me and made me feel sad. Mom would say you're depressed, that you need to take calcium and vitamin B and trace elements. She always thinks there's a solution to everything, you just have to find the right answer, have the knowledge. I'd really love her to be right but I think she's wrong. There isn't a cure for everything.

Reading your e-mail, I felt completely powerless. I'd like to find a magic formula so that you could have your own state like I've got mine and so we could live in peace. At peace. With a ban on news programs and bulletins and "we interrupt this program . . ." You talk about radios and TVs being on all the time; I know all about that. It's like a humming but also a hammering— you feel trapped by the words and images.

Yup, I'd really like that magic formula, I'd be prepared to pay for it too! But I'm not naive. I'm taking my exams this year, and I know that history is relentless; it doesn't think about people who want a quiet life, it just grinds on, sometimes destroying everything in its way.

Let's not talk about history then. Not today when what I really want to do is to thank you for giving me your name, your trust. Thank you for remembering my name is Tal. Thank you for telling me about your wonderful grandmother. Next time I go to Jaffa I'll look at the houses in a different light; I'll think about her and about you.

I want to ask you all the questions you haven't answered again: How old are you? What do you do?

Are you a student? Do you have a job? You told me you worked in Israel: Where? When? How did it feel?

I'd like to send you something of me too. A photo. It was taken last year on a school trip to Galilee. We walked for a whole day with backpacks on. Our guide, Oded, was hilarious. Something caught his eye every couple of minutes, and he'd kneel down in front of every flower and quote passages from the Bible that mentioned that type of flower. He also told us about a Jewish revolt in one particular village in Roman times; he couldn't stop saying, "I hope you realize how lucky you are. You're walking on land laden with history." Efrat sniggered because Shlomi had stepped on an anthill and took a while to notice. Anyway, it's a picture taken after a day of sweating in the sun, my hair's a mess, and I'm not wearing the sort of stuff I'd wear to go out in the evening, but I feel as if it's really me, that it shows me as I am most of the time. So you can put a face to my name.

I did some location work for the documentary this afternoon. I went to the film library. I love that place— they show old films in the original language or new films you can't see anywhere else. Last week I saw *Roman Holiday* with Gregory Peck and Audrey Hepburn. They're both so gorgeous! I'd love to look like her but, as you can see from the photo, I've got a long way to go . . . It's a great love story about a princess and a journalist. She's run away from the castle to live a normal life for a few days. It's very funny because it's really like she's come from another planet, she doesn't even know you have to pay in shops! But the ending's sad. I won't tell you what happens because you might see the film one day and, like me, you'll keep hoping right up to the last minute that the writer will take pity on sensitive souls and decide to opt for a happy ending with the closing shot.

Ori said I was like a little girl. That films with happy endings are for children in grade school, dribbly old women, and the incurably naive. I told him that in real life things often end badly, especially in our part of the world, so we need films to give us a bit of hope and just to *believe* that happy endings are possible.

Anyway, that's not important, I'll get back to the film library. It's a beautiful stone building with a restaurant on a terrace. It's separated from the Old Town and the Citadel of David by a little valley planted with olive trees, with the ruins of Sultan Suleiman's swimming pool. You can see the roofs of a monastery from there. Viewed from that side of the valley, the Old Town looks very sure of itself, completely calm, a long, long way from all those men fighting over it. For a few moments I tried to imagine what Jerusalem would be like with no inhabitants, with just the stone houses, the light, the warmth, the smells. It made my head spin.

Look at me! I'm taking over from my father: I'm going to be a guide to Jerusalem, for you, at least.

I haven't got school tomorrow (the teachers are on strike). I'm going to go to Rehavia where my grandparents live, my father's parents. Another hidden bit of paradise in Jerusalem.

That's enough for today. I can't wait to hear from you. Thanks again for everything you wrote to me. And if you're still sad and tired, do what I do when I feel like that: I put on my favorite record, lie down on my bed, and close my eyes. It works better than vitamin B.

Speak to you soon,

Tal

Naïm

She just keeps on with her offensive without even realizing it. She's good for me and she's bad for me. I'm only just balancing on a tightrope: toppling into the light on one side or, on the other, into murky darkness where there's no hope. When her message popped up I could feel my heart beating in my head. Well, to begin with, that's impossible; there is no way your heart can beat in your head. But why was something thumping inside my skull then?

I know exactly what it was, but I don't want to write it down. Anyway, I think more quickly than I can write, I have trouble keeping up. For a quarter of a second I tell myself, "I want to see her. Face-to-face. In flesh and blood." Then the next quarter second I hear myself saying, "You're talking nonsense. You think you're falling ~~in love~~, but it's just because you can't erase the memory of the other one."

To top it off, she's sent me her photo. Now that made a

whole lot of stuff happen at once too, in the split second that it took to open the file. I remembered how I'd hoped she would be ugly, but I was also afraid she really would be. I was worried I'd see a 250-pound monster with piggy eyes buried in the folds of her face, and then I was afraid she would be too gorgeous, too perfect. A miracle: she's simply pretty. Not bad. The sort you can walk past without noticing but if she smiles you've had it, and she's got a very nice smile in the picture. Head tilted to one side, an open angular face like someone really happy and healthy. Long, smooth chestnut-brown hair, greenish-brown eyes, a few freckles, fair skin. She's looking right into the lens. I'm in deep, it felt like it was me she was looking at, right in the eye. I'm sure that's why she chose that photo. So I looked at her too, for a moment, to etch her face in my memory, then I clicked delete. It tugged at something deep inside me but there's nothing else I can do. A guy next to me in the Internet café was giving me odd looks. I really didn't like it. I shut down my e-mail quickly and typed Audrey Hepburn into the search engine. Yup . . . she's very pretty with her cat's eyes and her dark bangs. But I didn't feel for one moment that she was smiling at me, not me specifically.

The guy wouldn't stop looking at me and he had a nasty glint in his eye. I tried to act casual and went on to the Al Jazeera site. At least everything's in Arabic there; it's completely above suspicion. I stayed on it for a quarter of an hour, reading all the news about the war in Iraq, a bomb in Saudi Arabia, and the children of the Jordanian royal family. Well, I say "reading" but I only really saw the headlines, clicking through them automatically, thinking about the film library in Jerusalem and how lucky she is to go off on school trips once a year. I finished off with a game of Tetris, which is a bit like a scan of my own brain at the moment: there are falling blocks that you have to try and line up in orderly rows, then the full rows disappear and leave room for more blocks.

I've decided not to go back to the Internet café. It's too dangerous. Especially at the moment, feelings seem to be running higher than ever. If anyone finds out I'm in contact with an Israeli girl who, rather than threatening or insulting, I'm thinking of as a friend, then my life's in danger, possibly my family's too. I've got to find another solution.

My father came home from the hospital exhausted. He's given up keeping track of his hours. He does the work of ten men, his eyes are constantly red. He slumped down on the sofa and said, "The day I work in a hospital where all my patients have cancer, heart complaints, or broken legs, then I'll know everything's fine, that our country's normal. For three years now we've been treating gunshot wounds and victims of missile attacks. When I decided to become a nurse, I thought I'd be relieving suffering that was inevitable, caused by mysterious disturbances in the body, not man-made ones. Who's going to stop this? And when?"

I wanted to tell him about Tal and her family. I wanted to tell him that there were people who'd had enough of this war on the other side too, people without hate. But I didn't dare. We don't often talk, the two of us. He hasn't been at home a great deal the last few years, they keep calling him in to do extra hours at the hospital. We've never talked much at home, anyway. After I was born my mother couldn't have any more children. There were plenty of people in the family who saw it as a curse, the evil eye on us. They gave my mother all sorts of advice to drive it away, and they wanted her to go to healers. Nothing did any good. I know some of them told my father to take another wife. He refused. At school they always gave me funny looks when I said I was an only child. My friends had at least eight brothers and sisters, sometimes ten or twelve. They couldn't believe I was all on my own, with a bedroom to myself. They all wanted to see it—my four walls, my bed, my desk, and my stuff—with their own eyes. At one point I thought of charging an entry fee. I could have gotten very rich, very quickly, but I didn't dare.

I've always thought my mother became a teacher to make up for all the children she didn't have because of me.

Why because of me?

It was as if I'd used up all her strength by coming into the world. She's got a tired face, my mom. Tired and beautiful. But maybe that's because life here is hard. Because we don't know anything, even the adults. We don't know if we'll be able to get to work, to eat when we want to, to sleep without the sound of explosions or helicopters roaring overhead. We don't know if the electricity's going to be cut off or the roads closed or if we're going to get to cousin Lubna's wedding in Rafah. (Rafah's not far away, ten miles or so. But if the Israelis decide that it will take six hours to travel ten miles, they know exactly how to go about it: they're the masters of time.) We don't even know if we'll be alive tomorrow.

I haven't thought about her for nearly twenty minutes. With a bit of practice, I might make it to thirty.

Right now I need to destroy everything. I'm going to tear these pages up into tiny pieces, into crumbs of paper, and flush them down the toilet.

Some Things Can't Be Described

From: Gazaman@post.com
To: bakbouk@writeme.com
Subject: Oh no!

Tell me you're all in one piece if you can.

I was at my uncle Ahmed's house this morning in Khan Younes. There were shouts of joy and cheering and people dancing. A bomb in al-Quds! *They* had managed to get through again! (Hamas or Jihad or el-Aqsa martyrs.) A bus had been blown up! Someone turned on the TV and switched to CNN. The carcass of a bus, ambulances, men rushing around, the usual. The reporter said the explosion happened not far from the prime minister's residence in Rehavia.

You said you were going to go there this morning, to see your grandparents. That's a problem. What I mean is, I would have a problem if anything happened to you. I don't know the others. Dead or alive, they don't matter to me.

Well, I don't know what else to say. I'm waiting to hear from you.

Naïm

From: Gazaman@post.com
To: bakbouk@writeme.com
Subject: (no subject)

I'm getting worried. You haven't replied for two days now. And you always write back really quickly, so something must have happened to you.

I hope it's nothing too serious.

Naïm

From: Gazaman@post.com
To: bakbouk@writeme.com
Subject: Phew!

Hi Tal,

At least I know you're not dead. I was particularly inspired, as you would say: I went on to an Israeli Web site that gave a list of victims of the bus bombing with the dates for their funerals. I read through it four times. There was a thirty-nine-year-old woman whose family said she was a great optimist; a social worker of Canadian descent; a French IT student; a thirty-eight-year-old Russian woman who—according to those who knew her—"loved people and life"; a twenty-three-year-old student; a forty-two-year-old man of Romanian descent whose wife described him as "a good person, a wonderful man, a good husband"; a

Russian woman of fifty-three, who no one knew much about; a former judo champion from Soviet Georgia; a twenty-four-year-old girl who'd been married for only a year; an Ethiopian woman who was working illegally; and a forty-eight-year-old man who'd just taken his wife to have a fertility test. And nowhere did the name Tal Levine come up (unless you lied to me about your name, but I'd be very surprised). They also said how many people were injured but didn't give any names: thirteen in serious or critical condition, thirty-seven with slight to moderate injuries. The site had a witness statement from a pharmacist who worked close to where the bus blew up. He said that it was horrible, terrible, there was blood everywhere . . . right, well, I'm sure you don't need me to give you the details, but I don't know what else to do except go on to Israeli sites and read everything I can about the explosion and zoom in on the pictures to see if I recognize your face at all.

And why aren't you writing to me, anyway? Why aren't you rushing to your computer? Why hasn't it occurred to you that I can worry too, about you? I can imagine things. I can almost imagine the worst. That someone close to you is dead or seriously injured. And that you hate me for it, me who hasn't done anything, that you hate all "the Palestinians," collectively guilty, every time. But what happened has nothing to do with me! Or my father, or my mother, or my uncle, Yacine's father, who definitely won't be losing any sleep over your victims but who didn't actually blow himself up in that bus! And we had some deaths too, last week, and we'll have more tomorrow, and next week, so what do you want? A competition to see which of us is suffering the most, who's crying the most? To score points? Go on then, get a calculator and all the newspapers for the last three years with the figures from all the confrontations between the Israelis and the Palestinians. Anyone with slight injuries = ten points. Moderate injuries = twenty points. Serious injuries = thirty points. Critical injuries = fifty points. And a death, ah, a death . . . Bingo! Jackpot! One hundred points!

I got angry, yet again. I often get carried away like that; it's like an engine and I have no control over the gears or the acceleration. Then it stops dead, I smack straight into a signpost. I'm sorry, please forgive me. Or think whatever you like. It's just unbearable not having any news of you, especially since I can finally get online without anyone watching me.

Yup, I haven't mentioned this to you: I was beginning to smell trouble at the Aman Internet café I was using so I had a brilliant idea, I went to the NGO just downstairs from my apartment. It's an Anglo-Italian organization that works with the psychology department at the hospital—they know my father well. I explained very nicely and very politely that I needed to go online but didn't really feel like going to an Internet café. They smiled and one of them said, "Okay, okay. You can come here. No problem." They kept giving me knowing winks, like they were thinking, "Yes, we're red-blooded men, too, we were young once, we understand why you'd want to go on to porn sites." They looked like extraterrestrials with their sunglasses pushed up onto their foreheads and their XXL-size smiles, but that wasn't important. What did matter was that they said I could come whenever I wanted and I could even help myself to their enormous stash of beer in the fridge. If we ever run out of everything here, they might die of hunger but never of thirst.

It's very nice being completely alone with a computer. I feel free, free, free as if I've been offered a square mile of open sky all to myself.

So, now that I just have to walk down three flights of stairs to pick up your e-mails or write to you, please do me a favor: be alive, be all in one piece, get back to your computer screen.

Naïm

From: bakbouk@writeme.com
To: Gazaman@post.com
Subject: Some things can't be described

Dear Naïm,

I'm so sorry. Sorry you were worried, sorry all this happened, sorry . . .

Unhappy, numb, gutted, that's how I feel. I haven't got the words, I can't find the right ones, I'm desperately short of them. I can't write what I have to say but I want to do it, so please forgive me if this isn't clear, forgive me if . . .

I can't do it. Even though YOU are the one person I really want to talk to about it. Because it was while I was reading your messages that I FINALLY managed to cry for the first time in three days. You have no idea how good it feels to cry, to sob, when the tears have been trapped in a solid block behind my forehead, a block that stopped me from talking or opening my eyes, or closing them, torturing me.

Thanks to you, I managed to cry. Thank you, Naïm. And even the bit where you "got angry," as you said, made me feel better, I can't explain why.

You guessed right: I was there, three days ago, at nine o'clock in the morning, when the number nineteen bus went up. I'm sure you know the name of the street: it was Gaza Street (!!!), in the lovely Rehavia quarter of Jerusalem.

I was there with my dad's camera. It was a beautiful cold morning. I wanted to film the bustle in the street first, and then turn left down Radak Street, which is always quieter, toward where my grandparents live.

I was walking along filming. I bumped into a man who was in a hurry and he shouted, "Hey, can't you watch where you're going?"

I thought I should erase the sequence, that some man in a hurry had no place in what I was doing.

I wanted to zoom in on a fat cat on the other side of the road, luxuriating in the sun as if he were on some peaceful Caribbean beach.

A bus came into the shot.

It never moved out of the shot. It never will.

I can't, I just can't describe what happened in the next second, and all the seconds after that.

I can't. I can't. I can't. The words have no meaning.

Terrible? It was worse than terrible. Horrendous? It was worse than horrendous. A nightmare?

No: hell. As if hell had suddenly sprung up from some invisible place and crashed down in the middle of the street.

I fell and the camera fell with me. I remember thinking, "Oh no, it's Dad's camera, he trusted me with it, he lent it to me, it mustn't break."

Afterward . . . no, I can't get it out, my heart's beating too fast, I mustn't. At the hospital they gave me tranquilizers or antidepressants or sleeping pills, I don't know, some sort of crap that was meant to help me get through the days ahead, but I don't want to take them, so I have to stay calm and be sensible. I mustn't let it all start bubbling away in my head or Mom will force me to take them.

I'll stop there for today. Sorry. I've only talked about myself. Sorry. I haven't even said I'm all in one piece. I'm not hurt, not even scratched, physically intact.

Speak to you soon, Naïm.

Tal

In Pieces

I'd like to not be me, for a while. To take a break from my own memory.

I started writing four months ago. After the explosion at the Hillel café I thought death had hovered over us and it would move on somewhere else after that.

But probabilities and statistics are only any good for math and biology, they're just numbers written on paper. What does it actually mean in real life if I have a one in three hundred thousand chance (Chance? I don't call that a chance!) to be within striking distance of a bomb twice in the space of four months?

So death hovered over me again, a bit closer this time, I felt its warm breath pick me up and drop me back down on the pavement. (I've always read that death was like a cold breath but it didn't feel like that on Gaza Street. It was hot, it even felt as if it was burning because the air around was so cold.)

Dad's camera has had it.

Apparently the tape inside it is unscathed, like me.

I've refused to watch it. Efrat and Ori told me I could offer it to a TV station, that I was bound to be the only person who filmed the explosion as it happened.

I didn't even answer.

Efrat realized that I resented them for having such a stupid idea.

"You know, Tal, we're not saying this because you could get money for it. I understand that you don't want to make money out of other people's suffering, but what you filmed there was news."

"Yes," Ori joined in, "it's live news. If you sold your tape to an agency it would be seen all over the world; it's really important."

"And why's it 'really important'?" I asked him (pretty coldly, I think).

"Because the whole world could finally see what we're going through here, what a bomb attack is like."

"Are you saying you know what it's like? You, Ori Sadé? I mean, I realize you actually do live in Jerusalem but you're not even old enough to vote! Have you ever seen a bomb blast up close? You think you know what it's like just because you turn on the TV every time something happens. But do you know something, Ori, the TV doesn't let you smell the smell, or hear the silence, that second of silence right after the explosion, the second when everyone's dazed, petrified. And then the screams, the moans, the sobbing, the groaning, they all cry like little children, the injured, even if they're fifty years old. And the TV won't show you them either, because it's not there yet, it's not 'at the bomb site' with its reporters all alive and unharmed and healthy, with its cameras and huge microphones. No one knows yet that this afternoon they'll be burying people who were heading off to work this morning, who'd paid their fare, a one-way ticket to death. Do you think they reimburse those tickets to the families? Shit, Ori! If you don't understand all that how do you expect the world to have the slightest idea of the hell it is? And, anyway, what difference does it make to us if the whole world knows and sees and understands? It won't change what's happened, or what'll happen tomorrow, here or in Gaza."

He looked embarrassed. And angry too. And all I wanted was to hurl myself at him, to hurt him and scratch him. To hurt my beloved Ori with his lovely hazel eyes and his soft curly hair and his beautiful hands like a pianist's—even if he does actually play the drums. To hurt my boyfriend who all of a sudden I couldn't stand the sight of.

My forehead was hurting, and my nose and upper lip. It's not as if I fell face first on the ground but I felt as if part of my face had tensed up, that it would never let me smile again or even just wear a normal expression.

Ori frowned.

"Why do you mention Gaza?"

"Did I mention Gaza?"

"Yes, you said, 'it won't change what'll happen tomorrow, here or in Gaza.'"

"Really? Well . . . people die every day—over there, over here, it never stops. And, in case you'd forgotten, Eytan's serving over there. I worry about him all the time."

He didn't seem convinced, but he didn't say anything. Efrat clearly picked up on something. She touched my arm and said, "I've got to go, Tal. I have to get my sister to daycare. Let's speak tomorrow?"

I nodded. I didn't feel like talking, but I tried to smile. She's a really good friend. For the last four days she's been asking every few hours how I'm feeling, right up until late in the evening, just before she goes to bed. She's brought me newspapers, books, Norah Jones's latest album, and a jasmine-scented candle.

"It's from my grandmother. She says jasmine calms the heart rate and drives away nightmares."

I held Efrat back and hugged her really tightly. She hugged me back and I could tell she had tears in her eyes. I don't know how we know that sort of thing without seeing, maybe because I had a prickling feeling in my own eyes and nose. She left my room and I heard her whispering with my mother in the corridor.

Ori was looking at me intently. I didn't want to meet his eye, I didn't want to hear him speak, and I certainly didn't want to hear the sound of my own voice. I closed my eyes. He came and sat on the edge of my bed, put one hand over mine, and with the other hand stroked my hair, sliding gently toward my temple until his hand was resting against my cheek, like a gentle shell fitting perfectly around my face, hardly moving his fingers. Tears spilled from my closed eyes one by one, tiny streams from a body of water that was overflowing inside, and they fell onto his fingers. He brushed them away gently, as if he felt some affection for them, as if he didn't want to hurt them, just to wipe them away.

I cried. For a long time. He put my head in the crook of his neck, in the place I've always called "my refuge." I cried for me, for him; for me because nothing's like it was before, not my love for him or the happiness I feel in his arms. I cried for the love he was giving me, wondering whether it wasn't a kind of betrayal, to be given so much tenderness without moving, without giving anything back in return. I cried because I felt so empty, alive but empty, fragile as an eggshell, hollow, with such a chasm inside me it makes me feel faint and sick. And all the time Ori went on gently massaging my head, without a word. It's so wonderful, someone who can say nothing like that, a boy who isn't afraid of being affectionate in silence.

And I thought back to how aggressive I'd been toward him, and I felt ashamed, so ashamed, but I couldn't bring myself to say sorry. I couldn't say anything, the tensing had reached down into my throat, and I just stayed in his arms, not moving, unable to say a single kind word or make one small gesture to show my gratitude.

He stayed until I went to sleep. Or rather he thought I'd gone to sleep, then he pulled away very slowly, put my arm down on the duvet, kissed my forehead, and went out on tiptoe.

A few minutes later my mother came in. She drew the curtains and stayed at the foot of the bed for a while. She heaved a sigh (of sadness or relief?).

Then I really did go to sleep.

I haven't set foot outside since they brought me home from the hospital on the evening of the twenty-ninth of January. I feel dizzy and can't walk properly; I want to stay in bed. They said I was in shock, that it would pass, that people who witness bombings always go through this.

I'm a watch that stopped at the time of the crime, a heart that carries on beating although the mind is no longer responding.

I cry, I stare into space, I see things I can't describe to anyone.

I keep thinking of Naïm. I really understand what he means when he says he's tired. I'm exhausted.

He was worried about me, like I was for him a while ago. But he was only worried about me, he said the others didn't matter to him. I would so like it if he could see this bombing as barbaric, terrible, and unforgivable like all the others. I'm beginning to understand that there are some kinds of pain that can't be shared. It's sad, but that's just the way it is.

That's a bit stupid, what I just wrote. I was worried about him too and *just* him, even if I did feel for all the others when I saw the destruction on TV. But that was so long ago . . .

It was before the twenty-ninth of January, before my eyes saw what they should never have seen.

Squirrels Don't Live in Gaza

From: Gazaman@post.com
To: bakbouk@writeme.com
Subject: What do I know? Who needs a subject?!

Good evening, Tal,

As you can see, I'm writing late at night. It's two in the morning. Willy and Paolo have gone home to bed but they've left me
the keys to their office. Willy and Paolo are the two guys from the
NGO who I made fun of the other day. I was wrong about them:
they're not clowns in sunglasses with mashed chickpeas between
their ears. They're good people. This afternoon they asked if I
wanted to go for a walk with them. We went to the old train
station, where the Cairo–Haïfa line used to pass before 1948. I
find it hard to imagine that people used to be so free to travel
here, without waiting on line for hours at some checkpoint. Anyway, there aren't any trains in the station now, there's a market.

Paolo wanted to buy a dress for his girlfriend, "a typical Palestinian one," he said with a smile. I was a bit surprised but I resisted the temptation to ask why a girl who lives in Rome and can buy all sorts of beautiful clothes would want to wear a dress from this place. He chose a red jellaba embroidered with silvery thread. It's lucky I was there because the stallholder tried to con him, asking for a hundred dollars, claiming the jellaba was hand-sewn using techniques that were over a thousand years old. I pointed out that the seams were very straight and regular and that if they hadn't been done by machine then Allah could turn me into a donkey on the spot. The man gave me a filthy look and said, "You stay out of this. It's nothing to do with you. I've got a family to feed. And a hundred dollars is nothing to your foreign friends."

Paolo decided to take care of the negotiating himself. He said he could pay sixty dollars if he got the dress as well as a little sky-blue jellaba for his cousin and three keffiyehs for friends. He told me you could get keffiyehs all over the place in Europe but these were the real thing because this is where they come from; he was sure his friends would like them.

Then we went along Omar al-Mukhtar Avenue and walked all the way to Rimaâl, the smart part of town along the coast, not far from where I found your bottle. (I know these place names don't mean anything to you, Tal, but I want you to know that the streets, the avenues, the districts, and the people have names here too. It's not just "the Gaza Strip.") It was already late. Paolo and Willy suggested eating in a restaurant. I was embarrassed because the restaurants around there are expensive and with what I had in my pocket, I could only afford a couple of mouthfuls of sparkling water and would look like a loser (which I probably am but I'd rather not everyone knew). I said I had things to do and I ought to get home.

But Willy said, "Hey, we'll treat you. It's my birthday today and I don't feel like celebrating it with this barbarian Italian who only drinks coffee and never tea." I thought Paolo would be upset, but he wasn't, so I said yes.

It was so good, Tal, you can't even imagine. The restaurant was hushed, they were playing a Natacha Atlas album very quietly, as if they wanted you to feel she was whispering in your ear. The waiters were well dressed and soft-spoken. I thought I'd been taken to paradise through a secret door. But when I saw the menu I thought, "If they use the same pricing system in paradise then there can't be many people there from where I come from." It was mind-blowing. There were dishes for ten, fifteen, even twenty dollars. And not even complicated things, the sort of stuff my mother does every day. Grilled lamb, eggplant with meat, hummus. Well, I think what you're paying for in that restaurant is something that's not actually on the menu: Feeling You're Somewhere Else, garnished with peaceful little vegetables and free-as-a-bird sauce.

Paolo and Willy ordered some wine. They asked if I drank alcohol. I said "yes, of course" very casually, as if I downed a bottle of whisky for breakfast every day, when I don't ever touch the stuff. They offered me a cigarette and that I did turn down. I mean, life expectancy's not great here as it is, but if I start inhaling poison too . . .

That really made them laugh. Willy looked at me as he

dragged on his cigarette and he asked, "What do you think about this situation, Naïm?"

I took a deep breath, opened my eyes wide, and puffed out my cheeks, sort of meaning, well, it's all pretty complicated.

"About what exactly?" I asked, playing for time.

"The intifada. The Israelis. The war."

I trotted out some bland replies, just like everyone else's: I want us to have our own state, I can't see why that's such a problem for the Israelis, but I don't know when it will happen because it's all gone so wrong even if Ariel Sharon has said he wants the Israelis to withdraw from the Gaza Strip. Then I asked them about themselves. I wanted to prolong the impression that we weren't in Gaza, I wanted them to take me away, to tell me about their countries, about England and Italy, and what their lives were like.

And they did take me away, Tal. And it was a hundred times better than doing it on the Internet. Willy told me incredible things about London. There's a park there where squirrels roam free. (Have you ever seen one? I haven't.) People walk around, sit on the grass, eat ice cream or popcorn, in families, in couples, or on their own. They read or chat or kiss, living their lives without worrying that some missile's going to land on them, without the radio announcing twice as much bad news as the day before, or a phone call telling them a brother, a cousin, or a friend has been injured or killed. He wasn't born in London—Willy, I mean—but he went to university there. He shared an apartment with three other students.

"Were they your cousins?" I asked him, and he burst out laughing.

"No!" he said. "I didn't know them. They put an ad for a share up in the university. I turned up, they gave me a room in the apartment, and we got to know each other afterward. Two girls, two boys. We got on well, except when the other boy had an eating binge in the night and raided the fridge . . . the others would yell at him the next day and make him pay back what the food had cost them, and he would call them uptight capitalist pigs."

I was flabbergasted. Here, you live with your family until you get married, and even afterward sometimes if there isn't enough money to rent or buy a house. So the thought of two girls who weren't even married living under the same roof with boys who weren't even their cousins . . . well, it was just impossible. Extraordinary and impossible.

They also told me about bars where people sing, and places you can go to dance, of little trips they went on as students all over the place: a few days in Paris, a few in Barcelona, a stint in Prague and Berlin. I thought they must be millionaires to have traveled that much, but I couldn't bring myself to ask them outright. So I asked what their parents did, and Willy said, "Mine run a grocery store in a village about fifty miles from London."

And Paolo said, "My father's an old hippie and I've probably only seen him ten times in thirty years. He sells goat cheese in market stalls in France. And my mother's a librarian."

Then, as if they'd guessed where my question was coming from, Paolo added, "Travel's not expensive in Europe, you know. You can go anywhere you like for fifty euros . . ."

I stared into my glass of wine so they wouldn't see I had tears in my eyes. There they were talking about all that freedom, all those journeys, and so many wonderful things, talking about it all so naturally that I thought they didn't even realize how lucky they were.

I had to bite my lip to stop myself from breaking down.

They pretended not to notice how I was feeling, managing somehow (how they did I have no idea) to make this look like politeness, not indifference. Willy started talking again.

"Paolo and I met in Rome, at a conference of organizations from all over the world. We saw the people from an organization called Free Speech, and they told us their aim was to set up teams of psychologists in every part of the world where there was suffering, so that they could listen to people."

Paolo took over then.

"You see, we can't stop the conflicts and we can't hand out money to everyone, but when we listen to people, when we help them find the hurt inside them, we can patch up the wounds a bit; we can do something to make them feei stronger, even in very difficult circumstances."

"What's really important," Willy added, "is for people to understand that they exist as individuals, that they're not just anonymous entities in a crowd where everyone's the same, just because they have a common fate. Each of them is unique."

It was devastating. The things they said churned me up inside. They said "listen," "patch up the wounds," "people exist as individuals," and every word they spoke melted down the blocks of ice inside me. I could feel the sobs rising up my throat, then they came up and turned into tears brimming in my eyes. I tried to contain them but it was too hard, I'd turned to liquid inside, I couldn't hold back the tears any longer.

I got up to go to the bathroom. Quickly.

Too quickly.

I knocked over my glass of wine and that made everything else spill out with it.

I broke down and cried. I buried my face in my hands. I wanted to stifle myself, to hide myself, to disappear. I was ashamed of who I am, so clumsy, and so weak, crying like that.

I'm twenty years old and there I was crying like a woman, like a child, like a madman, in front of two guys ten years older than me who'd invited me to a really expensive restaurant.

Willy put a hand on my shoulder. No one had done that to me since my grandmother died. I went to pieces, pathetic, ridiculous.

Paolo said we should go out and get some air.

I walked out with my head down, making a silent but very sincere promise to myself, on my parents' lives, that I would never set foot in that part of town again, or that restaurant, even if I was offered a private house on the dark side of the moon.

We walked toward the sea without a word. I kept sniffing and cursing myself for not having a hankie, for being me. Willy handed me one and said quietly, "You can talk if you want, Naïm."

And I talked like I've never talked to anyone, like you do possibly only once in a lifetime. I told those guys I hardly knew things I'd never told anyone. They listened and their eyes were intent and calm, as if they were saying, "Go on. We can hear it all. We've got as long as it takes. We won't judge you or tell anyone anything you say to us."

I don't know if I told them much about the "hurt I have inside," as they call it. But I told them about *me*, almost from the beginning.

110

And now I'm telling you about my evening, Tal, instead of writing it down on a piece of paper that I would then tear up.

I really need to tell someone that, for the first time in ages, ages and ages, I feel good.

Light.

Go on, I'm going to dare say it:

Happy.

Good night. I mean it this time.

Naïm

Jumping off a Roller Coaster,
Even at Full Speed

From: bakbouk@writeme.com
To: Gazaman@post.com
Subject: I'm here too!

Dear Naïm,

Look at the time. I'm not asleep either. I sat down to write to you and found the message you sent a few minutes ago. It was so simultaneous that I felt you were here with me, or not far away anyway, and I could see you for the first time. I couldn't describe you but I'm sure I'd recognize you in a crowd.

If you're still online, could we talk?

Let me know,

Tal

From: bakbouk@writeme.com
To: Gazaman@post.com
Subject: Another time . . .

You must have gone to sleep.

It doesn't matter; it feels as if you're still there, or you're there at last.

It's because it's late at night, and because of what you wrote too.

I love being awake at night. I feel a hundred times more alive than the rest of the time, and I can hear the voice inside my head more clearly, full of the emotions that can't cope with the light of day.

And, as Efrat says, most teachers sleep at night, and parents—that's why we feel freer!

So you're twenty years old, like my brother.

And you often have a lump in your throat, like me.

That was a good word, the word "happy" at the end of your e-mail. I wanted to cut out the bit of screen it was written on and hang it above my bed. Too bad monitors are so expensive . . .

I was at the station with you and Paolo and Willy, I walked along Omar al-Mukhtar Avenue. Your new friends took you to London and Rome, and you took me around Gaza. Thank you! (As for squirrels, I've never seen any either, except for in cartoons like *Bambi*.)

I haven't been out of the house or to school for a week. Efrat brings me the work I'm missing, but I don't look at it. We've got our midterms soon, but whether or not I pass seems such a tiny thing to me now. I feel I've been pulled apart. I can't focus or concentrate on anything or anyone for more than ten seconds.

Except your e-mails.

And in Ori's arms too, sometimes.

The rest of the time I'm on a roller coaster, going up and down at breakneck speed, not even sure which way up I am, whether it's me who's upside down, or the ride, or the world. All of me hurtling around dangerously fast.

Or rather, all my thoughts are hurtling around dangerously fast, bashing into each other, scattering about inside my head like ball bearings thrown into a magnetic field.

There it is: I saw bodies, dead people, things I don't want to describe. You gave me your name, Naïm, your trust. I heard screams, I didn't know human beings could produce noises like that. I should shut up now, I haven't got anything coherent to say. I want to gather myself together again, I'm like a ball of mercury that's broken up into tiny frantic little pieces. And it's all the Palestinians' fault because they don't want peace, they hate us, and all they care about is killing us. No it's not, it's our fault because for years we've refused them the right to their own state, but by what right do we refuse them that right? I'm getting bogged down, I'm floundering, my thoughts are like some manic rap song. I put Norah Jones on. I try to listen, to concentrate. At least she sounds happy and calm. I read the lyrics to the first song. For one whole line it goes *Ooooo, oooo, oooo*. It doesn't look like much—maybe just a stupid succession of zeros, but when it's her voice singing *Ooooo, oooo, oooo* it takes you far away, alone with a guitar you'd like to know how to play, on a cloud. But no, I can't concentrate on Norah Jones any longer than that. How about a DVD? I've seen *Dances with Wolves* six times in a week, and it's three hours long! The first time I watched it I thought my father could have played Kevin Costner's part. He moves in the same calm way, he has that same look in his eye that makes me melt with happiness because it makes me feel small and protected. No, no DVD. If I go to the living room my parents will know I'm awake and they'll force me to go back to bed. Funny, maybe I don't really want to feel so small and protected. I'm going to be eighteen soon. I'm even supposed to be going off on my national service in a few months' time. But no one's going to want me there if they realize I'm on a roller coaster the whole time.

I'd really like to see you, Naïm. For real, in the flesh. We'd have so much to say to each other. We could invite your friends Paolo and Willy along, and I'd introduce you to Efrat and Ori and Ori's sister. We'd find a quiet place in the Judean desert, by the

Dead Sea, you know, where it feels like you've been projected onto the moon without realizing it, the lowest point on earth. That's just what we need, the lowest point on earth, for a big party. It would be for all of us who refuse to be buried in this deep pit. Oh, it would be so good, Naïm, to eat and drink together, and Ori could bring his guitar, and we'd all go *Ooooo, oooo, oooo* like Norah Jones. We'd sing in Hebrew, in Arabic, in English, in Italian, and afterward I would bully you all into leaving the place spotless. The Dead Sea's sacred, it's completely unique, and I have been a member of EcoPeace for eight years.

Hey, maybe you have come back to your computer? It's four in the morning, but I'm not sure you're asleep after your traumatic evening. They're very kind to have left you the keys, those two.

Come on, be there!

Tal

From: bakbouk@writeme.com
To: Gazaman@post.com
Subject: Obviously . . .

I waited five minutes. Then ten. But you didn't come back down to check your e-mails, not that it was actually logical for you to come down at half past four to check your e-mails. You must be tossing and turning in bed, thinking over everything you said to Willy and

Paolo, and thinking about me too, perhaps. I'm sure I'm right about this. Tal's not crazy, you know, she's just a bit damaged, but she knows how other people feel. At least for the last few days, since your last e-mail, I feel I've got a real connection with you. And do you know what? I bet your parents were angry with you when you got home because you hadn't told them you'd be out so late . . .

I'm going to try and undo my seat belt and jump off the roller coaster without hurting myself. I'm going to try and sleep.

Good night, Naïm.

Tal

From: Gazaman@post.com
To: bakbouk@writeme.com
Subject: Your insomnia

Hi, Tal,

I'm worried about you. You're completely wired. You should see someone like Willy or Paolo—a psychologist, I mean. It would do you good. You can do that sort of thing easily in your country. It's more complicated here. Willy and Paolo told me they spend the most incredible amount of time trying to persuade people it's normal to go and see a psychologist. No one wants to send their children, especially their daughters. They're worried that if anyone knew, the girl would be labeled as insane and even a one-eyed hunchback wouldn't want to marry her. That's why the people from Free Speech do consultations in hospitals. Then people can say they're going to have their heart checked or have a blood test or go to visit someone when actually they're slipping through a back door and having their hurt patched up, as Willy calls it.

To change the subject, you were quite right, my parents were sick with worry and furious when I got home. I told them I was a man not a little boy. They told me the streets of Gaza were never safe, even for a man. I said that they wouldn't understand, that I'd been somewhere else. Or maybe that should be Somewhere Else, with capital letters, in a place where nothing could happen to me. They told me I was rambling, I was delirious, I'd been drinking, look, my shirt was even stained.

"Blood!" my mother screamed.

"No, it's wine," my father corrected her. "Your son's been drinking wine."

I told them I'd only had a mouthful and I wasn't rambling. I'd been with Willy and Paolo and they could ask them whether I'd made a fool of myself.

The scene ended with them promising me a present: yes, they want to give me a cell phone so they can get hold of me wherever and whenever they want.

I wanted to say I didn't need it and that soon they wouldn't need to worry about me.

But I didn't say anything.

They looked so reassured suddenly by their ingenious idea that they weren't angry anymore.

I've got to go now.

But before I do . . . you've given me an idea. Let's connect to

118

an instant messaging service. I imagine you know how to. Put me on your contacts list and I'll do the same. Then we'll really be able to talk . . .

Bye,

Naïm

Peace Comes from Insanity

Gazaman: Is that really you there, Tal? Is that you online?

Bakbouk: Yes, it's me

Gazaman: Are you okay?

Bakbouk: I don't know, and you?

Gazaman: I don't know either

Bakbouk: My parents had the same idea as you. They took me to see a therapist. I hadn't been out of the house for ten days and they said it couldn't go on any longer

Gazaman: What's your therapist like?

Bakbouk: He looks like John Lennon, from the Beatles

Gazaman: I know who you mean, my parents really like them. How's it going?

Bakbouk: Well, I couldn't say a single thing to him for ten minutes. I kept saying "er . . . um . . . well" and it was even worse trying to look him in the eye

Gazaman: And?

Bakbouk: He said "tell me what's going on inside your head"

Gazaman: And what did you tell him?

Bakbouk: I gave him a suspicious look and said it was a jumble inside my head: there was honey and vinegar, violins and heavy drums, rapping and Gregorian chants. I told him that if I gave him the whole list, even with operating instructions so he could understand it all, he'd have me locked away

Gazaman: Did you really think he would?

Bakbouk: Of course. Haven't you ever thought you were going crazy?

Gazaman: Lots of times

Bakbouk: You see! But maybe we're the normal ones, the ones who think they're going nuts

Gazaman: Yes. We should set up an Israeli–Palestinian asylum, you and me. It would be a beautiful symbol of reconciliation, as Westerners say. We could call it the Majnun & Meshuga Institute, with our motto engraved over the door: Peace comes from insanity

Bakbouk: That's brilliant! I've got to go, Ori's just arrived. Shall we try and talk again this evening?

Gazaman: I don't know if I'll be able to

Bakbouk: Why?

Gazaman: Because you never know what might happen. And even if you're not a believer, it's best to keep saying *Insha'Allah*

Bakbouk: We'll talk again this evening, *Insha' Allah*. Okay?

Gazaman: It seems strange, hearing it like that, from you. But it's okay

The same evening

Bakbouk: Hi Naïm
Gazaman: Hi Tal
Bakbouk: Do you spend all your time holed up in Paolo and Willy's office now?
Gazaman: Well I am at the computer quite a bit
Bakbouk: What do your two friends look like?
Gazaman: Why do you ask?
Bakbouk: Just because. I'm quite a visual person. Don't forget I wanted to be a filmmaker
Gazaman: Why do you say that in the past tense?
Bakbouk: Because I don't know what I want anymore. I managed to put two whole sentences together for John Lennon: "I somehow escaped death. And the thought of it keeps me awake."
Gazaman: Why does it keep you awake?
Bakbouk: Because I don't understand fate like that. If I'd been where the cat was, the one I was filming, I'd be dead
Gazaman: Did it really get killed?
Bakbouk: Yes
Gazaman: But it was just a cat. I mean: a cat's more fragile than a human being. You might only have been injured
Bakbouk: I'm not so sure about that. Anyway, what do Willy and Paolo look like?

Gazaman: Like Europeans

Bakbouk: What does that mean?

Gazaman: They look happy and relaxed even when they're unshaven. They're not constantly on the alert, ready to run at any moment. Willy's blond, quite tall, a bit like a young Bill Clinton. And Paolo . . . I don't know, it's completely meaningless describing people

Bakbouk: Fine. What about you?

Gazaman: What about me?

Bakbouk: What do you look like, who do you look like?

Gazaman: An Arab born of a man and a woman

Bakbouk: Hmm. Are you making fun of me again?

Gazaman: Maybe I am. If everyone pussyfoots around you you'll never get out of Gaza Street. You'll be stuck there for the rest of your life with the dead cat and the debris of that bus

Bakbouk:

Gazaman: Why the silence?

Bakbouk: I'm crying. I'm smiling. You're better at this than John Lennon!

Gazaman: No. He's doing a job. I know you from before

Bakbouk: Do you really feel you know me?

Gazaman: Yes and I can see you too. I can really see you, I've got that photo of you in my head. I never had time to thank you for it, it was just before the bombing. You're . . . pretty. Congratulations

Bakbouk: I had nothing to do with it! "We choose none of the things that determine our lives: not the way we look or where we're born or our parents. None of them. We just have to cope with all the things we haven't

123

chosen and that make us who we are." My father told me that last year, when I was having trouble with just being me. (By the way, it was a terrorist attack on Gaza Street, not a bombing)

Gazaman: If you like. Our two nations have never agreed on words. You say Israel, we say Palestine. You say Jerusalem, we say al-Quds. You say you're "hunting down terrorists in Sichem" and we say you're "hot on the heels of our fighters in Nablus" (and it's the same town and the same men!). You say a terrorist and we say a martyr (if he's dead, obviously, otherwise he's a fighter, a courageous fighter). You say "let's start with security, and then there will be peace" and we say "let's start with peace, and security will happen of its own accord." In fact, before setting up our asylum for Israeli and Palestinian psychotics, we should make a bi-national dictionary to agree on the words we use, your people and mine. (And your father's an intelligent man)

Bakbouk: I think if we could agree on words we could agree on everything

Gazaman: Not a bad idea, not bad at all. Must go now. I've got something important to do

Bakbouk: What?

Gazaman: It's a secret

Bakbouk: You have lots of secrets, don't you?

Gazaman: No, I mostly have dreams. But at the moment I want to keep them secret

Bakbouk: Will you tell me them one day?

Gazaman: Maybe. Bye

Eytan's Revelations

From: bakbouk@writeme.com
To: Gazaman@post.com
Subject: Tons and tons of unbelievable news

Dear Naïm,

I haven't been able to go online for a few days. I couldn't get to my mailbox. When I got into it I thought I might find a handful of e-mails from you (obviously from you, you're the only person who knows this address). There was nothing. And the little window that usually shows when you're connected at the same time as me won't open. What's going on?

I know it's quiet in Gaza at the moment. Well, they haven't announced anything particular on the radio.

Let's say you're up to some secret mission and you'll resurface sooner or later.

I've got lots of things to tell you. Tons and tons. I don't know where to start!

I go to see John Lennon twice a week. Ever since he smiled and said he didn't need an instruction manual to understand me, I tell him everything that comes into my head without even editing it, and it's very relaxing. I don't know if it's "helping," as they say, but at least it's getting me out a bit and I'll be going back to school soon. Sometimes I go out in the evening with Ori; I get as far as his house—it's not very far—walking along the street holding his arm and feeling like a little old lady. I remember reading in the paper a few months ago about all the victims who are never mentioned: the ones who witness bombings without actually being injured, or only very slightly, but who are still traumatized, frozen in time and paralyzed with fear. There was a couple saying how they no longer had a life since their children witnessed a bombing on their way to a shopping center. They had to drive them to school in the car, and pick them up by car too. The mother stopped work so she could chauffeur them around. At home the children insisted the door be locked and the shutters closed all the time. They refused to let their parents go out in the evening, even if they had a babysitter. They slept with the light on and frequently woke in the night. "Our life's over," the mother kept saying. "We'll only be saved when the children can cope with having the shutters open."

In another newspaper, *Haaretz*, there was an article about Palestinian children last week. Now sit up and listen to this closely, it's unbelievable. Eighty percent of them have been injured or traumatized by an act of war they've witnessed or been affected by in some way. The journalist mentioned how difficult it would be to get all of them to see a psychologist, and he quoted one Paolo Fraterini of Free Speech!!! Can you believe it! Your friend Paolo here in my country, in my living room! Well, on the table in the living room. I was so happy, I had to tell someone. Eytan was at home. (He's not in Gaza anymore. He's doing one last training session somewhere in the north of the country, then he'll be free. Almost at exactly the same time as I'll be setting off, if they think I'm fit for service, which is far from guaranteed . . .) Anyway, Eytan was at home, and I told him everything. What was in the bottle, us e-mailing each other, you. He didn't seem surprised. I shook him and said, "Eytan, I tell you I've got a Palestinian friend and this is your only reaction?"

"I sort of knew."

"WHAT?"

"What did you expect? When you gave me your bottle, I had to open it. I had to know what was inside it."

"But . . . why?"

"Do you live on Mars or something? Did you really think I'd throw a bottle in the Gaza Sea, without knowing what was inside it? I'm a soldier, Tal. Not some irresponsible dreamer!"

"Oh, so that's what I am, that's what you're saying. I'm irresponsible and crazy, is that it?"

He told me he didn't think that at all, that he'd done it first and foremost to protect me, but I wasn't listening, I was yelling at him that he'd betrayed me, and that I'd never trust him again.

Our apartment is big, but not so big you couldn't hear me shouting at the other end. I don't scream very often, I hate that sort of thing, it's just that, when I actually do it, you can hear me in the Old Town.

My parents came running.

"What on earth are you two up to? You're behaving like little children!" my mother said.

"It's him! It's him! He betrayed me!" I screamed, pointing at Eytan.

"What do you mean?" Dad asked calmly.

So I told them everything, stammering my way through it. They looked stunned.

"So what? I haven't done anything wrong. You're the ones who brought me up thinking the Palestinians are our equals, you can't exactly blame me for wanting to get to know them better!"

I'll spare you the details. They told me that, far from being annoyed, they thought what I'd done was beautiful, even if it could have been dangerous. ("What if your bottle had ended up with a fanatic? He could have hurt you with what he said, with all that hatred.") They were surprised I hadn't told anyone about it, especially Dad. I told them that it had to be a secret, that I didn't want it to be a family thing, for people to keep asking me about it. They asked me about you. I couldn't tell them much. What I know about you can't really be summed up. I told them you're twenty, you live in Gaza, and you write well.

Eytan asked, "Is that all you can tell us about him?"

Yes, it's all.

My father said that our correspondence was a sign of hope. That it proved something was possible between you and us, a human exchange, friendly, even. You see where I get it from, all that optimism . . .

Later Eytan came to my room. I was sitting on the floor staring at a large fan spread out above my bed. Ori's sister brought it back from Thailand for me a year ago. It's got big black birds on it, just about to take flight, but they never actually fly. There are also clumps of flowers, not flowers that I've ever seen, and no one here knows what they're called.

Eytan sat down next to me. He put his arm around my shoulders gently.

"Are you still annoyed with me, little sister?"

I waggled my head to mean both yes and no.

"I wanted to protect you, just to protect you. You don't know what Gaza's like. There are so many people on that little strip of land! People like you and me, only even worse off because they're not so free, because there are constant curfews, because there's a very high unemployment rate, because they're fed up with their lives. And then there are the others, the fanatics: they're terrifying. I wanted to be sure your bottle had a chance of getting into the right hands."

"But how?"

"I half buried it in the sand. Then I went and checked the spot at regular intervals to see if it was still there or if someone had taken it. On the sixth day a young guy came and sat down on the beach, alone. He was holding a book, but not reading. He looked at the sea and the sky for a long time, then he lay down and—"

"YOU SAW NAÏM? And you didn't talk to him? You didn't say anything to him?"

"We hadn't exactly been introduced, you know."

"What's he like? Describe him!"

"Quite tall. Probably nearly six foot. Slim. He was wearing jeans and a blue T-shirt. Short, slightly curly hair. Nothing very distinctive, and I was too far away to see the color of his eyes."

(You're right, Naïm, descriptions don't mean anything. But can you believe it! My brother saw you!)

Then I asked him what happened and he said you opened the bottle, took out the letter, and read it. Several times, he thought. He said you lay down for a while, then put the bottle in your bag.

"And then?"

"That's all."

"What do you mean, that's all?"

"He left with the bottle. I have no idea why, but I trusted him. Because he was on his own and he looked out to sea and was carrying a book."

"Didn't you follow him?"

"I'm not a private detective! I'm a soldier. You can't wander around Gaza City in an Israeli uniform all by yourself like a tourist."

I was so overwhelmed! And not angry at all anymore. My brother had seen you. He had trusted you.

He was right.

Oh, I feel you're so close now. It seems more and more unreal, more and more illogical that we can't meet!

Write to me!

Speak to you soon,

Tal

A Jacket for Protection

Ori couldn't come to see me this evening. He was invited to a wedding and I didn't feel like going with him. I couldn't handle dancing or loud music but what I really couldn't cope with was six hundred people all having fun.

My father asked whether I'd like to go out for a bit of a walk with him, as a substitute for my daily little old lady's walk with Ori.

We started off along Emek Refaïm Street, heading toward the film library. As we passed the Hillel café I shuddered: six months ago a young woman was sitting at a table there with her father and then . . .

I turned to my own father, who was good and alive beside me, and said, "Do you remember Nava Appelbaum?"

He frowned and tilted his chin toward the café.

"The girl who died here with her father six months ago?"

"Yes, the one who was supposed to be getting married the next day."

"I remember. Why do you ask?"

"Well, it was after that bombing that I started writing, that I thought of putting everything in a bottle, and I gave the bottle to Eytan."

"I understand what you were doing," my father murmured.

"Really?"

"Of course. Your survival instinct took over that day. Whether or not you did it consciously, you were defending yourself against despair. You wanted to go beyond the violence, to speak in a language different from that of hate or indifference. I think that any normal human being needs to know they're not surrounded by enemies waiting to pounce."

I sighed. I started shaking, with cold, or something else. My father put his jacket over my shoulders. I huddled inside the thick, rough fabric, breathing in the smell of him, and I felt sort of protected.

"You know, Dad, I feel so much older than I did six months ago . . ."

He nodded and asked, "What does 'old' mean to you?"

"I don't know how to explain it . . . I don't feel like making any plans or thinking about the future. I saw with my own eyes a bus full of people who all had plans and . . ."

"Yes?"

". . . those plans went up with everything else."

He didn't say anything. He put his arm around my neck. The walls of the Old Town were suddenly there, facing us, and—without even saying a word—we sat down on a bench and looked at them.

The ramparts were floodlit, making rectangles of crenellated light, and to the left was the Citadel of David (which does not date back to David's time, my father usually adds), rising serenely toward the moon.

As if reading my thoughts, my father said, "Scenery can be soothing. It can go beyond our suffering because it's so vast it gives us back our sense of proportion."

It was true. I felt very small. But that was also because of the jacket.

"Do you see that?" my father went on. "It's quite rare for the moon to be directly over the Citadel of David, which actually—"

"—doesn't date back to David's time and which was extensively restored by Suleiman the Magnificent in the sixteenth century, I know!"

We burst out laughing.

It was the very first time since the twenty-ninth of January. My whole body shook, exactly halfway between laughter and tears. It wasn't unpleasant.

I could tell my father wanted to know more about Naïm, but he didn't dare ask. So, once I calmed down, I said, "You know, six months ago when I sent my bottle, I was very naive. I really thought Eytan would throw it into the sea; I wanted a real miracle to happen. I told myself that if someone found it and wrote to me, then that would be a sign in itself."

"A sign of what?" he asked.

"That there's no frontier that can't be crossed."

"And did you cross it, this frontier?"

"I think so. Well, it didn't go at all as I expected. I was convinced it would be a girl, that we would tell each other about our lives, and, through that, I would get a feel for a whole nation. It wasn't like that. I'm sure it's better this way. I don't think I know the Palestinians any better—it doesn't make much sense trying to do that, short of moving over there for a few months and living their lives. I think I know Naïm. But more than that: I care about him. At one point I even thought I was falling in love with him! Oh, I know it's easy getting carried away with things on the computer, but I liked reading his e-mails, I was always impatient for the next one, and I reread them again and again. He made me laugh a lot, including when he was making fun of me. And the rest of the time, he touched me, because he didn't write like other boys, who don't write much anyway. Because he trusted me too, eventually."

"And what about Ori in all this?"

"I love him. Well, I think I do. But then if someone told me I could go to Gaza now, this minute, without running any risks, I'd go straight to see Naïm. And the fact that it's impossible hurts, it really hurts."

"It's impossible *now*, Tal. But it might not always be."

I looked up at him.

"Aren't you fed up with believing that, Dad?"

"Believing what?"

"That there'll be peace between us and the Palestinians. You must have been fighting for it for thirty years now, and it's just going from bad to worse."

"Thirty years isn't much in history. You'll see when you really *are* old!"

He was smiling but I could see he was cold. If I'd offered his jacket back he would have refused it so I stood up.

As we walked he whispered, "Keep all your dreams intact, Tal. Dreams are what get us somewhere. Don't stop believing and wanting what you've always wanted . . . whether that's making films or peace or whatever."

His voice was gentle. It felt as if it were opening up pathways inside my head, bringing fresh oxygen to my brain in the little place (right hemisphere? left hemisphere?) that can imagine the future.

Just before going back up to the house, I said, "The fact that I care about Naïm makes me happy and sad. Happy because it's wonderful to have such a normal kind of contact with someone from over there, it warms me just like this jacket. And sad because . . ."

"Because?"

"I haven't heard from him for several days. I'm worried something serious has happened to him. I've been listening to the radio and they haven't announced any deaths or anything over there, but in one of his e-mails he said something like: 'Soon my parents won't have to worry about me.' That's a terrible thing to say, isn't it? Surely it is worrying. Maybe he's going to . . . to do something drastic. Well, I don't know. I'm frightened for him, Dad."

The Whole Truth

Bakbouk: You're there, Naïm, I know you are. You've just come online. Can we talk?

Gazaman: Sorry. What I want to tell you is too long. I'm going to write you an e-mail. Be patient, this could take a while. Don't hate me for it.

From: Gazaman@post.com
To: bakbouk@writeme.com
Subject: Telling you everything at last. Then . . .

Dear Tal,

This will be my last letter to you, and please, please don't reply to it, don't write to me anymore after this.

It's exactly six months since I found your bottle. Happy anniversary to the two of us!

I've liked being Gazaman, the guy you knew nothing about,

who made fun of you, and was sometimes angry but still knew that you'd read what he said without hating him. But we can't control everything, even on a computer, and without even realizing it, you found exactly the right way to get to Naïm.

My name is Naïm Al-Farjouk. I was born in Gaza twenty years ago. My father's a male nurse and my mother's an elementary school teacher. They couldn't have any more children after me. I'm one of the very few only children in the Gaza Strip, perhaps even the only one.

My parents have really spoiled me, really loved me. And I was very good at school too, if you must know. In the message in the bottle you talked about your dreams, saying you wanted to be a film director or pediatrician. I've always dreamed of being a doctor. I like the way they take an interest in you, tilting their heads and asking such precise questions as they try to understand what's wrong with you. And when they pick up their pens to write the prescription, you always feel that's it, they've found the solution and everything's going to be fine. Doctors are magicians, and I really like the idea of performing miracles.

When I was little (and even quite recently too) I would close my eyes and try to think of something with all my strength to make it happen. It worked once or twice, but I knew even then that it was only coincidence. Eventually I realized that you had to roll up your sleeves and get on with it to make miracles happen.

When Yasser Arafat came to Gaza in 1994 my father came into my room with a book in his hand and said, "Naïm, you're going to learn Hebrew. We're going to be at peace with the Israelis and that's a good reason to learn their language properly." So every evening after I'd finished my homework I studied the *Aleph Beth* and everything about your language, which is so like my own. I very quickly learned the conjugations by heart, and I got into the habit of watching Israeli television to get better and expand my vocabulary.

At the very beginning you said you could picture young Americans really clearly because you saw them in TV series. For me it was like that with you, the Israelis. I got to know you through TV. And one day I felt like taking it further. It was the summer of 2000, I was seventeen, I didn't want to hang around in Gaza for a whole boring summer, and I wanted to earn some money. I asked my parents if I could go and work in Israel. They hesitated, out of pride I think. They earned a good enough living for their son to not need to be a laborer in Israel. But I insisted and they agreed.

I had to get up early, three in the morning, to get to the border crossing at Erez. My father took me. He was a bit sad but I was more excited: it felt like an adventure. I waited in line for two hours with other young people and men trying to earn enough to feed a family. They were poor and tired and all seemed to know each other. I didn't have anyone to talk to but I liked being on my own; it didn't bother me. On the other side of the crossing point there were Israeli buses. An Israeli told me he was looking for people to work on a building site. He asked me if I could paint, do a bit of glazing, tiling, plumbing, and wiring. I'd once helped my parents repaint our apartment so I said yes. The bus set off for Tel Aviv. Everyone went to sleep except for me—I kept my eyes wide open so I didn't miss a single detail.

At first I was a bit disappointed: there were big gray fields; it was pretty much like Gaza. Then we got to the outskirts of Tel Aviv. I was surprised because the road signs were written in Hebrew, English, and Arabic. It felt like home but somewhere else.

The cars on the roads were as beautiful as the ones used by the Palestinian authorities, but the houses were definitely bigger, taller, whiter. I noticed lots of gardens with things for children.

Coming into Tel Aviv I saw huge buildings, real skyscrapers. I decided I'd have to find a way of going to the top of one sometime, to see what it was like.

The man who took me on was named Avi. He told me he'd pay me a hundred shekels for a day's work if the work was good. I thought: how strange, I'll be earning more than my father.

On the way to the site I drank in everything I saw. I could have done with a thousand pairs of eyes. Shops like nothing I'd ever seen, hairdressing salons that looked like cafés, restaurants that looked like museums . . . I'd have liked to leave Avi there and go for a stroll but that wasn't an option.

I prayed he'd give me an easy job, thinking that even if he did find out I'd lied, he couldn't take me straight back to Gaza and at least I'd get one day's holiday in Israel. When we got to the apartment we were going to be working on he said, "Here, you, you can paint the kitchen, it needs a second coat."

I put on the overalls he gave me and started carefully painting with a roller. Someone put on the radio, there was great music, and we worked like that all morning. Now and then I glanced out of the window. I saw children going off to school, old people out for a walk, women doing their shopping or chatting on their cell phones while they waited for the bus. It was so much calmer and more peaceful than Gaza that it made me sad. Still, I was happy to be there too. At lunchtime the others took pita bread and fruit out of their bags. I hadn't brought anything to eat, and I didn't have any money on me. Avi shouted out, "Hey, new boy, are you planning to work on an empty stomach?" I was embarrassed but he took my arm and said, "Come on, we'll go down and get you something."

I followed him, thinking he talked just like my uncle Hassan, my mother's younger brother who went to live in Canada.

The rest of the day went very quickly. Avi took us back to the meeting point where the bus was waiting for us. He handed me my money and said, "You worked well. Come back tomorrow."

A month went by like that. Every morning and every evening I felt I was going through an invisible curtain and crossing from one dimension to another. Gaza, Tel Aviv. Tel Aviv, Gaza. How can I describe what separates the two cities? In Gaza there's all the noise of the crowds. In Tel Aviv it's the cars. In Gaza the streets are full of men. In Tel Aviv there are girls, on their own or in groups, heads held high. The air smells different. Maybe because there are more trees and cars and restaurants and money. Maybe it's the women's perfume or sunscreen from people on the beaches. Every morning and every evening I thought I must be covering at least six thousand miles, that these two cities couldn't possibly be just forty miles apart.

Avi was kind. One day he saw me reading a newspaper someone had left lying around and he said, "Your Hebrew's very good, isn't it? Can you read it too?" I told him my father had taught me.

He looked surprised but didn't say anything else.

Another time he asked me to lay some turquoise floor tiles in a bathroom. It was a beautiful building in the north of Tel Aviv. I admitted I'd never laid tiles in my life. "So did you lie to me on the first day?" he asked. I looked down. I don't like the word "lie" and I didn't want him to use it in connection with me. I thought he'd be angry and send me away but he took my shoulder and said, "Come on, I'll show you. It's not rocket science so long as you've got two good hands. But I'll pay you a bit less today because I'm giving you training that could be useful for the rest of your life and could earn you a lot of money if you work well."

One evening when four of us were working at a site, Avi asked us to stay. The Gaza Strip had been sealed off during the day and he couldn't handle things without us the next day. He said he'd rather pay a fine for letting us stay in Tel Aviv than get behind with the job. The other three said yes right away; they seemed to be used to staying overnight in Israel. I muttered something about letting my parents know. He took out his cell phone so I could call them.

My mother didn't want me to stay. She was afraid I'd be arrested because after eight o'clock in the evening Palestinians aren't allowed to be on Israeli soil. I told her not to worry and that the boss knew what he was doing.

Avi brought sleeping bags and sandwiches, then turned to me.

"Naïm, you're pretty young to sleep on site. You can come home with me if you like."

I looked at the other three to see what they thought. They shrugged, and I left with Avi.

That evening I went into an Israeli home for the first time. Avi introduced me to his wife, Osnat, and his daughter, Tal. He told me his eldest son was on national service, over in Hebron, in an Israeli–Palestinian patrol. At the time, if you remember, we were right in the middle of negotiations for a definitive ruling: Yasser Arafat and Ehud Barak were meeting Bill Clinton at Camp David to finalize the agreement.

There was almost peace and, most important, independence for us.

But I wasn't thinking about all that. I was in an Israeli house and I felt great, too much so.

We all ate together. Avi's wife and daughter asked me lots of questions about Gaza and my family. They commented on my Hebrew, saying I spoke better than plenty of Israelis and didn't make any mistakes. I was quite proud. At the end of the meal Avi said, "Roll on peace, once and for all, Naïm. Our two nations should be able to live together just like us around this table this evening."

Then Tal asked if I'd like to watch TV with her. There was a game show called *Who Wants to Be a Millionaire?* I could answer almost all the questions. Tal said, "You should phone in to take part!" I told her I wasn't at all convinced a Palestinian could take part and she said that would all change soon.

Over the next few weeks I often stayed the night with them. It felt like a vacation, but I was working very hard. It was like staying with rich, good-natured cousins who wanted to share everything with me. I liked their bathroom, their leather sofa, the miniature plates Osnat collected, their smiles, the way they held out their hands to me and said, "Shalom, Naïm."

And then I fell in love with Tal.

She had very short blond hair, a little ski-jump nose, a funny way of sitting cross-legged that I really liked.

When I talked to her she didn't look away like the girls do here.

She made lots of jokes and puns. She burst out laughing so easily and she was a karate black belt. She wore shorts, sandals, and tank tops. She had three earrings in her right ear and one in her left.

Sometimes she would play CDs for me in her room. Sometimes friends of hers would come around and stay for the evening or go out with her. Some of them talked to me quite naturally, others were wary of me.

One day she told me I'd look better without my mustache, it made me look old. She laughed and said it made me look like an actor in an Egyptian film!

I shaved it off the next day.

I couldn't wait for the evenings when Avi invited me home. I didn't want to go back to Gaza anymore. I didn't talk to my parents much; all I could think about was her, her and Tel Aviv. A girl and a city who were both free.

I don't think she was in love with me, but she really liked me—she told me I was more patient than her brother . . . that was enough for me.

At the end of August I couldn't imagine life without seeing Tal. That was when Yasser Arafat and Ehud Barak came back from America without having reached an agreement. I heard people talking about it; I'd stopped listening to the news. My father looked worried, but I didn't really think about it. We're so used to our independence being put off, delayed, postponed, that the day it actually happens we'll all have heart attacks, so it could wait a bit longer.

In September Tal went back to school. She was in her last year. I'd finished high school and didn't want to go to college right away. I told my parents I'd work in Israel for another year to save money for when I was a student.

One evening Tal got annoyed because she just couldn't solve a math problem. I said I might be able to help her. It was the same syllabus as ours and it was all fresh in my mind. It was easy helping her. She was really pleased. We stayed in her room a long time that evening, listening to music, talking, and not talking. She smiled at me so softly. She told me she'd had a boyfriend but he'd left her when he went on national service because he'd met another girl there. She told me she always wondered whether she'd know the love of her life when she met him, and whether there was such a thing as "the love of your life." I said I had no idea. I wanted to tell her that when your heart beats in a particular way and you toss and turn in bed in a particular way and can't sleep, when you're sometimes really hungry and sometimes not hungry at all, when you stop thinking about other people and yourself, then that must be love. I hesitated for a while and then I told her.

She looked at me with that little smile.

"You've got the softest heart, Naïm."

My legs were shaking. I said I had to go to bed, that I had to be up early for work.

146

Then there was no work for a few days and I stayed in Gaza, just doing nothing and thinking of her.

I could have looked for work with someone else but that didn't appeal to me at all.

In Gaza people were getting angry, saying Yasser Arafat had been wrong to trust the Israelis and that negotiating with them would never work.

On the twenty-ninth of September 2000 a series of confrontations broke out between Palestinians and your police in Jerusalem. There were some casualties, a few deaths. The second intifada had just started.

I won't tell you the rest; you know it as well as I do. Or rather you know all about the events that affected Israelis, and I know all about events that have harmed Palestinians.

The Gaza Strip was closed off for a long time. Then there were more and more bombings in Israel and boys my age were no longer allowed to go and work there.

I never saw or heard from Tal, Avi, and Osnat again.

So I made the only sensible decision: I promised myself I'd get away from here. I'd leave this bloody place to live a free life in a free world, in a world where no gunshot would stop me being with who I want to be with, where and when I want.

I took my father's books and studied so hard, I drowned myself in them. My mother's brother, Hassan, told me that if I got high enough grades I could get a grant to study in Canada. I managed to get not just high grades but excellent ones. I filled in forms and applied by letter. I lived in hope. And despair too.

I got the answer today: I got accepted.

I'm shaking with excitement. For a few years I'm going to have the right to live like Paolo and Willy. I'm going to become a doctor. Then I'll come back to this country I was born in. I hope, I so hope things will have changed, that we'll have our own state, that ambulance sirens will only wail for car accidents and heart attacks. But, for now, I only want to think of me. Just me.

I loved reading your e-mails and writing to you, Tal. Now you may see why it hasn't always been easy for me to do it, and not for political reasons.

You're a good person. Generous. And fragile.

Of course we can carry on writing to each other, the Web means we can, but I want to wipe these last few years from my memory for a while, and you're a part of them. I want to be brand new over there, in Canada. Not to be connected to this land that shakes day and night, this land that stops people from sleeping and thinking of themselves. One day your people and mine will realize no one can possibly win with violence, that it's a loser's war. A waste.

But I won't forget you altogether, Tal.

You once said you have to say everything twice with me. It's true.

So you and I are going to try and do the miracle of the bottle a second time. I'm taking it with me, and I'll make a date with you for three years' time, for the thirteenth of September 2007, at midday, in Rome, by the Trevi Fountain. Paolo's told me a lot about the place, and it will be a reminder of the Audrey Hepburn film you went to see at the film library. I'll have your bottle under my arm. Very romantic, don't you think? But I like the idea; I'm even impatient for an opportunity to be romantic.

In three years, that's a promise.

Till then, I hope all goes well for you,

Naïm